DIESTERWEGS NEUSPRACHLICHE BIBLIOTHEK

Seize the Day

by
SAUL BELLOW
Winner of the 1976 Nobel Prize for Literature

Edited and annotated
by
Gerd David

VERLAG MORITZ DIESTERWEG
Frankfurt am Main · Berlin · München

4075

DIESTERWEGS NEUSPRACHLICHE BIBLIOTHEK

Englische Abteilung

Eine Sammlung englischer und amerikanischer Lesestoffe für das 5. bis 9. Unterrichtsjahr, herausgegeben von Johannes Schütze

CONTENTS

ISBN 3-425-04075-8

1. Auflage

Verlag Moritz Diesterweg GmbH & Co., Frankfurt am Main, 1979
Alle Rechte vorbehalten. Die Vervielfältigung auch einzelner Teile, Texte oder Bilder –
mit Ausnahme der in §§ 53, 54 URG ausdrücklich genannten Sonderfälle –
gestattet das Urheberrecht nur, wenn sie mit dem Verlag vorher vereinbart wurde.

Gesamtherstellung: Oscar Brandstetter Druckerei KG, Wiesbaden

INTRODUCTION

I was the man, I suffer'd,
I was there.

Walt Whitman

The Author, his Works and Themes

Saul Bellow was born in 1915 in the Canadian province of Quebec. His
family, of Russian-Jewish origin, had emigrated from St. Petersburg to
Canada two years before. However, Bellow spent his youth in Chicago,
where he grew up in a multi-lingual environment (English, French,
Yiddish, Hebrew).

He studied anthropology and sociology at three American universities, but he did not finish his post-graduate studies because he had
found out that his research kept turning into fiction. "In my innocence I
had decided to become a writer."

After establishing a certain reputation as a novelist Bellow was
appointed to the teaching-staff of several universities in various
positions: Assistant Professor of English, Professor of Creative
Writing, Visiting Lecturer. He is currently teaching literature to a select
group of graduate students in the social sciences at the University of
Chicago.

For his writing he has received a number of national book awards.
After a series of very successful novels, which won him wide
recognition, he was awarded the Nobel Prize for Literature in 1976.

"Every writer ought to try to reach as many people as he possibly can.
A writer should simply assume that an enormous number of readers will
understand him. . . . At this hour of civilization we had better assume
that we can speak out." Although Bellow is regarded by some critics as a
novelist of the intellectuals, he has always succeeded in addressing a
wider public because of the relevance of his themes and the variety of his
literary styles. His novels, in chronological order, are:

Dangling Man (1944)   *Henderson the Rain King (1959)*
The Victim (1947)   *Herzog (1964)*
The Adventures of Augie March (1953) *Mr. Sammler's Planet (1970)*
Seize the Day (1956)   *Humboldt's Gift (1975)*

In addition to these, Bellow has published a collection of short stories, plays, a range of articles on cultural and literary criticism and, recently, a report on his visit to Israel *(To Jerusalem and Back: A Personal Account, 1976)*.

Bellow's themes, however dissimilar his novels may be in stylistic respects, embrace a central idea: the suffering individual, confused and threatened by the chaos of contemporary life, finds himself in search of some understanding that will enable him to accept and affirm his existence. After a variety of experiences the victims, "apprentices in suffering and humiliation", reach this point of acceptance and are left, in one way or another, with a gleam of hope.

Bellow has often expressed his strong disagreement with ideas of nihilism and alienation that are characteristic of modern literature. His optimism – disguised as it may be – has been interpreted as accommodation and cheap compromise. A discussion of any of his novels will have to take this argument into consideration.

Thus, Bellow's heroes have the two faces of victim and survivor. The author's personal background (as the son of Jewish immigrants) explains his frequent choice of Jews as his heroes; but, more than that, the Jew is the prototype of the suffering human being. Above all, it is the *schlemiel* type of Jewish folklore that often appears in the wide range of Bellow's heroes (cf. Tommy Wilhelm in *Seize the Day*). He is the victimized figure that attracts misfortune, and in this hostile environment the *schlemiel* tries to find a standard by which he is able to live. In his search he is frequently confronted with powerful theoreticians, eccentrics, would-be teachers, confidence men, who try to dominate, and take advantage of, the hero (cf. Dr. Tamkin in *Seize the Day*).

The Swedish Academy, which selected him as the Nobel Prize winner, praised Bellow's portrayal of "a man who keeps on trying to find a foothold during his wanderings in a tottering world, one who can never relinquish his faith that the value of life depends on its dignity, not its success . . ."

Note: The *Study Questions* following the text of the novel are intended to direct your attention to some specific problems of understanding the text. They are supplemented by the more general *Questions for Discussion* and some excerpts from *Critical Comments*.

SEIZE THE DAY

I

When it came to concealing his troubles, Tommy Wilhelm was not less capable than the next fellow. So at least he thought, and there was a certain amount of evidence to back him up. He had once been an actor – no, not quite, an extra – and he knew what acting should be. Also, he was smoking a cigar, and when a man is smoking a cigar, wearing a hat, he has an advantage; it is harder to find out how he feels. He came from the twenty-third floor down to the lobby on the mezzanine to collect his mail before breakfast, and he believed – he hoped – that he looked passably well: doing all right. It was a matter of sheer hope, because there was not much that he could add to his present effort. On the fourteenth floor he looked for his father to enter the elevator; they often met at this hour, on the way to breakfast. If he worried about his appearance it was mainly for his old father's sake. But there was no stop on the fourteenth, and the elevator sank and sank. Then the smooth door opened and the great dark red uneven carpet that covered the lobby billowed toward Wilhelm's feet. In the foreground the lobby was dark, sleepy. French drapes like sails kept out the sun but three high, narrow windows were open, and in the blue air Wilhelm saw a pigeon about to light on the great chain that supported the marquee of the movie house directly underneath the lobby. For one moment he heard the wings beating strongly.

Most of the guests at the Hotel Gloriana were past the age of retirement. Along Broadway in the Seventies, Eighties, and Nineties, a great part of New York's vast population of old men and women lives. Unless the weather is too cold or wet they fill the benches about the tiny railed parks and along the subway gratings from Verdi Square to Columbia University, they crowd the shops and cafeterias, the dime stores, the tea-rooms, the bakeries, the beauty parlours, the reading rooms and club rooms. Among these old people at the Gloriana, Wilhelm felt out of place. He was comparatively young, in his middle forties, large and blond, with big shoulders; his back was heavy and strong, if already a little stooped or thickened. After breakfast the old guests sat down on the green leather armchairs and sofas in the lobby and began to gossip and look into the papers; they had nothing to do but wait out the day. But Wilhelm was used to an active life and liked to go out energetically in the morning. And for several months, because he had no position, he had kept up his morale by rising early; he was shaved and in the lobby by eight o'clock. He bought the paper and some cigars and drank a Coca-Cola or two before he went in to breakfast with his father. After breakfast – out, out, out to attend to business. The getting out had in itself become the chief business. But he had realized that he could not keep this up much longer, and today he was afraid. He was aware that his routine was about to break up and he sensed that a huge trouble long presaged but till now formless was due. Before evening, he'd know.

Nevertheless he followed his daily course and crossed the lobby.

Rubin, the man at the news-stand, had poor eyes. They may not have been actually weak but they were poor in expression, with lacy lids that furled down at the corners. He dressed well. It didn't seem necessary – he was behind the counter most of the time – but he dressed very well. He had on a rich brown suit; the cuffs embarrassed the hairs on his small hands. He wore a Countess Mara painted necktie. As Wilhelm approached, Rubin did not see him; he was looking out dreamily at the Hotel Ansonia, which was visible from his corner, several blocks away.The Ansonia, the neighbourhood's great landmark, was built by Stanford White. It looks like a baroque palace from Prague or Munich enlarged a hundred times, with towers, domes, huge swells and bubbles of metal gone green from exposure, iron fretwork and festoons. Black television antennae are densely on its round summits. Under the changes of weather it may look like marble or like sea-water, black as slate in the fog, white as tufa in sunlight. This morning it looked like the image of itself reflected in deep water, white and cumulous above, with cavernous distortions underneath. Together, the two men gazed at it.

Then Rubin said, "Your dad is in to breakfast already, the old gentleman."

"Oh, yes? Ahead of me today?"

"That's a real knocked-out shirt you got on," said Rubin. "Where's it from, Saks?"

"No, it's a Jack Fagman – Chicago."

Even when his spirits were low, Wilhelm could still wrinkle his forehead in a pleasing way. Some of the slow, silent movements of his face were very attractive. He went back a step, as if to stand away from

6

himself and get a better look at his shirt. His glance was comic, a comment upon his untidiness. He liked to wear good clothes, but once he had put it on each article appeared to go its own way. Wilhelm, laughing, panted a little; his teeth were small; his cheeks when he laughed and puffed grew round, and he looked much younger than his years. In the old days when he was a college freshman and wore a racoon coat and a beanie on his large blond head his father used to say that, big as he was, he could charm a bird out of a tree. Wilhelm had great charm still.

"I like this dove-grey colour," he said in his sociable, good-natured way. "It isn't washable. You have to send it to the cleaner. It never smells as good as washed. But it's a nice shirt. It cost sixteen, eighteen bucks."

This shirt had not been bought by Wilhelm; it was a present from his boss – his former boss, with whom he had had a falling out. But there was no reason why he should tell Rubin the history of it. Although perhaps Rubin knew – Rubin was the kind of man who knew, and knew and knew. Wilhelm also knew many things about Rubin, for that matter, about Rubin's wife and Rubin's business, Rubin's health. None of these could be mentioned, and the great weight of the unspoken left them little to talk about.

"Well, y'lookin' pretty sharp today," Rubin said.

And Wilhelm said gladly, "Am I? Do you really think so?" He could not believe it. He saw his reflection in the glass cupboard full of cigar boxes, among the grand seals and paper damask and the gold-embossed portraits of famous men, Garcia, Edward the Seventh, Cyrus the Great. You had to allow for the darkness and deformations of the glass, but he thought he didn't look too good. A wide wrinkle like a comprehensive bracket sign was written upon his forehead, the point between his brows, and there were patches of brown on his dark blond skin. He began to be half amused at the shadow of his own marvelling, troubled, desirous eyes, and his nostrils and his lips. Fair-haired hippopotamus! – that was how he looked to himself. He saw a big round face, a wide, flourishing red mouth, stump teeth. And the hat, too; and the cigar, too. I should have done hard labour all my life, he reflected. Hard honest labour that tires you out and makes you sleep. I'd have worked off my energy and felt better. Instead I had to distinguish myself – yet.

He had put forth plenty of effort, but that was not the same as working hard, was it? And if as a young man he had got off to a bad start it was due to this very same face. Early in the nineteen-thirties, because of his striking looks, he had been very briefly considered star material, and he had gone to Hollywood. There for seven years, stubbornly, he had tried to become a screen artist. Long before that time his ambition or delusion had ended, but through pride and perhaps also through laziness he had remained in California. At last he turned to other things, but those seven years of persistence and defeat had unfitted him somehow for trades and business, and then it was too late to go into one of the professions. He had been slow to mature, and he had lost ground, and so he hadn't been able to get rid of his energy and he was convinced that this energy itself had done him the greatest harm.

"I didn't see you at the gin game last night," said Rubin.

"I had to miss it. How did it go?"

For the last few weeks Wilhelm had played gin almost nightly, but yesterday he had felt that he couldn't afford to lose any more. He had never won. Not once. And while the losses were small they weren't gains, were they? They were losses. He was tired of losing, and tired also of the company, and so he had gone by himself to the movies.

"Oh," said Rubin, "it went okay. Carl made a chump of himself yelling at the guys. This time Doctor Tamkin didn't let him get away with it. He told him the psychological reason why."

"What was the reason?"

Rubin said, "I can't quote him. Who could? You know the way Tamkin talks. Don't ask me. Do you want the *Trib*? Aren't you going to look at the closing quotations?"

"It won't help much to look. I know what they were yesterday at three," said Wilhelm. "But I suppose I better had get the paper." It seemed necessary for him to lift one shoulder in order to put his hand into his jacket pocket. There, among little packets of pills and crushed cigarette butts and strings of cellophane, the red tapes of packages which he sometimes used as dental floss, he recalled that he had dropped some pennies.

"That doesn't sound so good," said Rubin. He meant to be conversationally playful, but his voice had no tone and his eyes, slack and lid-blinded, turned elsewhere. He didn't want to hear. It was all the same to him. Maybe he already knew, being the sort of man who knew and knew.

No, it wasn't good. Wilhelm held three orders of lard in the commodities market. He and Dr. Tamkin had bought this lard together four days ago at 12.96, and the price at once began to fall and was still falling. In the mail this morning there was sure to be a call for additional margin payment. One came every day.   5

The psychologist, Dr Tamkin, had got him into this. Tamkin lived at the Gloriana and attended the card game. He had explained to Wilhelm that you could speculate in commodities at one of the uptown branches of a good Wall Street house without making the full deposit of margin legally required. It was up to the branch manager. If he knew you – and   10
all the branch managers knew Tamkin – he would allow you to make short-term purchases. You needed only to open a small account.

"The whole secret of this type of speculation," Tamkin had told him, "is in the alertness. You have to act fast – buy it and sell it; sell it and buy it again. But quick! Get to the window and have them wire Chicago at   15
just the right second. Strike and strike again! Then get out the same day. In no time at all you turn over fifteen, twenty thousand dollars' worth of soy beans, coffee, corn, hides, wheat, cotton." Obviously the doctor understood the market well. Otherwise he could not make it sound so simple. "People lose because they are greedy and can't get out when it   20
starts to go up. They gamble, but I do it scientifically. This is not guesswork. You must take a few points and get out. Why, ye gods!" said Dr Tamkin with his bulging eyes, his bald head, and his drooping lip. "Have you stopped to think how much dough people are making in the market?"   25

Wilhelm with a quick shift from gloomy attention to the panting laugh which entirely changed his face had said, "Ho, have I ever! What do you think? Who doesn't know it's way beyond nineteen-twenty-eight – twenty-nine and still on the rise? Who hasn't read the Fulbright investigation? There's money everywhere. Everyone is shovelling it in.   30
Money is – is –"

"And can you rest – can you sit still while this is going on?" said Dr Tamkin. "I confess to you I can't. I think about people, just because they have a few bucks to invest, making fortunes. They have no sense, they have no talent, they just have the extra dough and it makes them   35
more dough. I get so worked up and tormented and restless, so restless! I haven't even been able to practise my profession. With all this money around you don't want to be a fool while everyone else is making. I

know guys who make five, ten thousand a week just by fooling around. I know a guy at the Hotel Pierre. There's nothing to him, but he has a whole case of Mumm's champagne at lunch. I know another guy on Central Park South – But what's the use of talking. They make millions. They have smart lawyers who get them out of taxes by a thousand schemes."

"Whereas I got taken," said Wilhelm. "My wife refused to sign a joint return. One fairly good year and I got into the thirty-two-per-cent bracket and was stripped bare. What of all my bad years?"

"It's a businessmen's government," said Dr Tamkin. "You can be sure that these men making five thousand a week –"

"I don't need that sort of money," Wilhelm had said. "But oh! if I could only work out a little steady income from this. Not much. I don't ask much. But how badly I need –! I'd be so grateful if you'd show me how to work it."

"Sure I will. *I* do it regularly. I'll bring you my receipts if you like. And do you want to know something? I approve of your attitude very much. You want to avoid catching the money fever. This type of activity is filled with hostile feeling and lust. You should see what it does to some of these fellows. They go on the market with murder in their hearts."

"What's that I once heard a guy say?" Wilhelm remarked. "A man is only as good as what he loves."

"That's it – just it," Tamkin said. "You don't have to go about it their way. There's also a calm and rational, a psychological approach."

Wilhelm's father, old Dr Adler, lived in an entirely different world from his son, but he had warned him once against Dr Tamkin. Rather casually – he was a very bland old man – he said, "Wilky, perhaps you listen too much to this Tamkin. He's interesting to talk to. I don't doubt it. I think he's pretty common, but he's a persuasive man. However, I don't know how reliable he may be."

It made Wilhelm profoundly bitter that his father should speak to him with such detachment about his welfare. Dr Adler liked to appear affable. Affable! His own son, his one and only son, could not speak his mind or ease his heart to him. I wouldn't turn to Tamkin, he thought, if I could turn to him. At least Tamkin sympathizes with me and tries to give me a hand, whereas Dad doesn't want to be disturbed.

Old Dr Adler had retired from practice; he had a considerable fortune and could easily have helped his son. Recently Wilhelm had told him, "Father – it so happens that I'm in a bad way now. I hate to have to say it. You realize that I'd rather have good news to bring you. But it's true. And since it's true, Dad – what else am I supposed to say? It's true." 5

Another father might have appreciated how difficult this confession was – so much bad luck, weariness, weakness, and failure. Wilhelm had tried to copy the old man's tone and made himself sound gentlemanly, low-voiced, tasteful. He didn't allow his voice to tremble; he made no stupid gesture. But the doctor had no answer. He only nodded. You 10 might have told him that Seattle was near Puget Sound, or that the Giants and Dodgers were playing a night game, so little was he moved from his expression of healthy, handsome, good-humoured old age. He behaved toward his son as he had formerly done towards his patients, and it was a great grief to Wilhelm; it was almost too much to bear. 15 Couldn't he see – couldn't he feel? Had he lost his family sense?

Greatly hurt, Wilhelm struggled however to be fair. Old people are bound to change, he said. They have hard things to think about. They must prepare for where they are going. They can't live by the old schedule any longer and all their perspectives change, and other people 20 become alike, kin and acquaintances. Dad is no longer the same person, Wilhelm reflected. He was thirty-two when I was born, and now he's going on eighty. Furthermore, it's time I stopped feeling like a kid towards him, a small son.

The handsome old doctor stood well above the other old people in 25 the hotel. He was idolized by everyone. This was what people said: "That's old Professor Adler, who used to teach internal medicine. He was a diagnostician, one of the best in New York, and had a tremendous practice. Isn't he a wonderful-looking old guy? It's a pleasure to see such a fine old scientist, clean and immaculate. He stands straight and 30 understands every single thing you say. He still has all his buttons. You can discuss any subject with him." The clerks, the elevator operators, the telephone girls and waitresses and chambermaids, the management flattered and pampered him. That was what he wanted. He had always been a vain man. To see how his father loved himself sometimes made 35 Wilhelm madly indignant.

He folded over the *Tribune* with its heavy, black crashing sensational print and read without recognizing any of the words, for his mind was still on his father's vanity. The doctor had created his own praise. People were primed and did not know it. And what did he need praise for? In a hotel where everyone was busy and contacts were so brief and had such small weight, how could it satisfy him? He could be in people's thoughts here and there for a moment; in and then out. He could never matter much to them. Wilhelm let out a long, hard breath and raised the brows of his round and somewhat circular eyes. He stared beyond the thick borders of the paper.

. . . love that well which thou must leave ere long.

Involuntary memory brought him this line. At first he thought it referred to his father, but then he understood that it was for himself, rather. *He* should love that well. "This thou perceivest, which makes *thy* love more strong." Under Dr Tamkin's influence Wilhelm had recently begun to remember the poems he used to read. Dr Tamkin knew, or said he knew, the great English poets and once in a while he mentioned a poem of his own. It was a long time since anyone had spoken to Wilhelm about this sort of thing. He didn't like to think about his college days, but if there was one course that now made sense it was Literature I. The textbook was Lieder and Lovett's *British Poetry and Prose,* a black heavy book with thin pages. Did I read that? he asked himself. Yes, he had read it and there was one accomplishment at least he could recall with pleasure. He had read, "Yet once more, O ye laurels." How pure this was to say! It was beautiful.

Sunk though he be beneath the wat'ry floor . . .

Such things had always swayed him, and now the power of such words was far, far greater.

Wilhelm respected the truth, but he could lie and one of the things he lied often about was his education. He said he was an alumnus of Penn State; in fact he had left school before his sophomore year was finished. His sister Catherine had a B.S. degree. Wilhelm's late mother was a graduate of Bryn Mawr. He was the only member of the family who had no education. This was another sore point. His father was ashamed of him.

But he had heard the old man bragging to another old man, saying, "My son is a sales executive. He didn't have the patience to finish school. But he does all right for himself. His income is up in the five figures somewhere."

"What – thirty, forty thousand?" said his stooped old friend.

"Well, he needs at least that much for his style of life. Yes, he needs that."

Despite his troubles, Wilhelm almost laughed. Why, that boasting old hypocrite. He knew the sales executive was no more. For many weeks there had been no executive, no sales, no income. But how we love looking fine in the eyes of the world – how beautiful are the old when they are doing a snow job! It's Dad, thought Wilhelm, who is the salesman. He's selling me. *He* should have gone on the road.

But what of the truth? Ah, the truth was that there were problems, and of these problems his father wanted no part. His father was ashamed of him. The truth, Wilhelm thought, was very awkward. He pressed his lips together, and his tongue went soft; it pained him far at the back, in the cords and throat, and a knot of ill formed in his chest. Dad never was a pal to me when I was young, he reflected. He was at the office or the hospital, or lecturing. He expected me to look out for myself and never gave me much thought. Now he looks down on me. And maybe in some respects he's right.

No wonder Wilhelm delayed the moment when he would have to go into the dining-room. He had moved to the end of Rubin's counter. He had opened the *Tribune;* the fresh pages drooped from his hands; the cigar was smoked out and the hat did not defend him. He was wrong to suppose that he was more capable than the next fellow when it came to concealing his troubles. They were clearly written out upon his face. He wasn't even aware of it.

There was the matter of the different names, which, in the hotel, came up frequently. "Are you Doctor Adler's son?" "Yes, but my name is Tommy Wilhelm." And the doctor would say, "My son and I use different monickers. I uphold tradition. He's for the new." The Tommy was Wilhelm's own invention. He adopted it when he went to Hollywood, and dropped the Adler. Hollywood was his own idea, too. He used to pretend that it had all been the doing of a certain talent scout named Maurice Venice. But the scout had never made him a definite offer of a studio connexion. He had approached him, but the results of the screen tests had not been good. After the test Wilhelm took the initiative and pressed Maurice Venice until he got him to say, "Well, I

13

suppose you might make it out there." On the strength of this Wilhelm had left college and had gone to California.

Someone had said, and Wilhelm agreed with the saying, that in Los Angeles all the loose objects in the country were collected, as if America had been tilted and everything that wasn't tightly screwed down had slid into Southern California. He himself had been one of these loose objects. Sometimes he told people, "I was too mature for college. I was a big boy, you see. Well, I thought, when do you start to become a man?" After he had driven a painted flivver and had worn a yellow slicker with slogans on it, and played illegal poker, and gone out on Coke dates, he had *had* college. He wanted to try something new and quarrelled with his parents about his career. And then a letter came from Maurice Venice.

The story of the scout was long and intricate and there were several versions of it. The truth about it was never told. Wilhelm had lied first boastfully and then out of charity to himself. But his memory was good, he could still separate what he had invented from the actual happenings, and this morning he found it necessary as he stood by Rubin's show-case with his *Tribune* to recall the crazy course of the true events.

I didn't seem even to realize that there was a depression. How could I have been such a jerk as not to prepare for anything and just go on luck and inspiration? With round grey eyes expanded and his large shapely lips closed in severity toward himself he forced open all that had been hidden. Dad I couldn't affect one way or another. Mama was the one who tried to stop me, and we carried on and yelled and pleaded. The more I lied the louder I raised my voice, and charged – like a hippopotamus. Poor Mother! How I disappointed her. Rubin heard Wilhelm give a broken sigh as he stood with the forgotten *Tribune* crushed under his arm.

When Wilhelm was aware that Rubin watched him, loitering and idle, apparently not knowing what to do with himself this morning, he turned to the Coca-Cola machine. He swallowed hard at the Coke bottle and coughed over it, but he ignored his coughing, for he was still thinking, his eyes upcast and his lips closed behind his hand. By a peculiar twist of habit he wore his coat collar turned up always, as though there were a wind. It never lay flat. But on his broad back, stooped with its own weight, its strength warped almost into deformity, the collar of his sports coat appeared anyway to be no wider than a ribbon.

He was listening to the sound of his own voice as he explained, twenty-five years ago in the living-room on West End Avenue, "But, Mother, if I don't pan out as an actor I can still go back to school."

But she was afraid he was going to destroy himself. She said, "Wilky, Dad could make it easy for you if you wanted to go into medicine." To remember this stifled him.

"I can't bear hospitals. Besides, I might make a mistake and hurt someone or even kill a patient. I couldn't stand that. Besides, I haven't got that sort of brains."

Then his mother had made the mistake of mentioning her nephew Artie, Wilhelm's cousin, who was an honour student at Columbia in maths and languages. That dark little gloomy Artie with his disgusting narrow face, and his moles and self-sniffing ways and his unclean table manners, the boring habit he had of conjugating verbs when you went for a walk with him. "Roumanian is an easy language. You just add a *tl* to everything." He was now a professor, this same Artie with whom Wilhelm had played near the soldiers' and sailors' monument on Riverside Drive. Not that to be a professor was in itself so great. How could anyone bear to know so many languages? And Artie also had to remain Artie, which was a bad deal. But perhaps success had changed him. Now that he had a place in the world perhaps he was better. Did Artie love his languages, and live for them, or was he also, in his heart, cynical? So many people nowadays were. No one seemed satisfied, and Wilhelm was especially horrified by the cynicism of successful people. Cynicism was bread and meat to everyone. And irony, too. Maybe it couldn't be helped. It was probably even necessary. Wilhelm, however, feared it intensely. Whenever at the end of the day he was unusually fatigued he attributed it to cynicism. Too much of the world's business done. Too much falsity. He had various words to express the effect this had on him. Chicken! Unclean! Congestion! he exclaimed in his heart. Rat race! Phony! Murder! Play the Game! Buggers!

At first the letter from the talent scout was nothing but a flattering sort of joke. Wilhelm's picture in the college paper when he was running for class treasurer was seen by Maurice Venice, who wrote to him about a screen test. Wilhelm at once took the train to New York. He found the scout to be huge and oxlike, so stout that his arms seemed caught from beneath in a grip of flesh and fat; it looked as though it must be positively painful. He had little hair. Yet he enjoyed a healthy complexion. His breath was noisy and his voice rather difficult and husky because of the fat in his throat. He had on a double-breasted suit of the type then known as the pillbox; it was chalk-striped, pink on blue; the trousers hugged his ankles.

They met and shook hands and sat down. Together these two big men dwarfed the tiny Broadway office and made the furnishings look like toys. Wilhelm had the colour of a Golden Grimes apple when he was well, and then his thick blond hair had been vigorous and his wide shoulders unwarped; he was leaner in the jaws, his eyes fresher and wider; his legs were then still awkward but he was impressively handsome. And he was about to make his first great mistake. Like, he sometimes thought, I was going to pick up a weapon and strike myself a blow with it.

Looming over the desk in the small office darkened by overbuilt midtown – sheer walls, grey spaces, dry lagoons of tar and pebbles – Maurice Venice proceeded to establish his credentials. He said, "My letter was on the regular stationery, but maybe you want to check on me?"

"Who, *me?*" said Wilhelm. "Why?"

"There's guys who think I'm in a racket and make a charge for the test. I don't ask a cent. I'm no agent. There ain't no commission."

"I never even thought of it," said Wilhelm. Was there perhaps something fishy about this Maurice Venice? He protested too much.

In his husky, fat-weakened voice he finally challenged Wilhelm, "If you're not sure, you can call the distributor and find out who I am, Maurice Venice."

Wilhelm wondered at him. "Why shouldn't I be sure? Of course I am."

"Because I can see the way you size me up, and because this is a dinky office. Like you don't believe me. Go ahead. Call. I won't care if you're cautious. I mean it. There's quite a few people who doubt me at first. They can't really believe that fame and fortune are going to hit 'em."

"But I tell you I do believe you," Wilhelm had said, and bent inward to accommodate the pressure of his warm, panting laugh. It was purely nervous. His neck was ruddy and neatly shaved about the ears – he was fresh from the barbershop; his face anxiously glowed with his desire to make a pleasing impression. It was all wasted on Venice, who was just as concerned about the impression he was making.

"If you're surprised, I'll just show you what I mean," Venice had said. "It was about fifteen months ago right in this identical same office when I saw a beautiful thing in the paper. It wasn't even a photo but a drawing, a brassière ad, but I knew right away that this was star material. I called up the paper to ask who the girl was, they gave me the name of the advertising agency; I phoned the agency and they gave me the name of the artist; I got hold of the artist and he gave me the number of the model agency. Finally, finally I got her number and phoned her and said, 'This is Maurice Venice, scout for Kaskaskia Films.' So right away she says, 'Yah, so's your old lady.' Well, when I saw I wasn't getting nowhere with her I said to her, 'Well, miss. I don't blame you. You're a very beautiful thing and must have a dozen admirers after you all the time, boy friends who like to call and pull your leg and give a tease. But as I happen to be a very busy fellow and don't have the time to horse around or argue, I tell you what to do. Here's my number, and here's the number of the Kaskaskia Distributors, Inc. Ask them who am I, Maurice Venice. The scout.' She did it. A little while later she phoned me back, all apologies and excuses, but I didn't want to embarrass her and get off on the wrong foot with an artist. I know better than to do that. So I told her it was a natural precaution, never mind. I wanted to run a screen test right away. Because I seldom am wrong about talent. If I see it, it's there. Get that, please. And do you know who that little girl is today?"

"No," Wilhelm said eagerly. "Who is she?"

Venice said impressively, "'Nita Christenberry."

Wilhelm sat utterly blank. This was failure. He didn't know the name, and Venice was waiting for his response and would be angry.

And in fact Venice had been offended. He said, "What's the matter with you! Don't you read a magazine? She's a starlet."

"I'm sorry," Wilhelm answered. "I'm at school and don't have time to keep up. If I don't know her, it doesn't mean a thing. She made a big hit, I'll bet."

"You can say that again. Here's a photo of her." He handed Wilhelm some pictures. She was a bathing beauty – short, the usual breasts, hips, and smooth thighs. Yes, quite good, as Wilhelm recalled. She stood on high heels and wore a Spanish comb and mantilla. In her hand was a fan.

He had said, "She looks awfully peppy."

"Isn't she a divine girl? And what personality! Not just another broad in the show business, believe me." He had a surprise for Wilhelm. "I have found happiness with her," he said.

"You have?" said Wilhelm, slow to understand.

"Yes, boy, we're engaged."

Wilhelm saw another photograph, taken on the beach. Venice was dressed in a terry-cloth beach outfit, and he and the girl, cheek to cheek, were looking into the camera. Below, in white ink, was written, "Love at Malibu Colony."

"I'm sure you'll be very happy. I wish you —"

"I *know*," said Venice firmly, "I'm going to be happy. When I saw that drawing, the breath of fate breathed on me. I felt it over my entire body."

"Say, it strikes a bell suddenly," Wilhelm had said. "Aren't you related to Martial Venice the producer?"

Venice was either a nephew of the producer or the son of a first cousin. Decidedly he had not made good. It was easy enough for Wilhelm to see this now. The office was so poor, and Venice bragged so nervously and identified himself so scrupulously — the poor guy. He was the obscure failure of an aggressive and powerful clan. As such he had the greatest sympathy from Wilhelm.

Venice had said, "Now I suppose you want to know where you come in. I seen your school paper, by accident. You take quite a remarkable picture."

"It can't be so much," said Wilhelm, more panting than laughing.

"You don't want to tell me my business," Venice said. "Leave it to me. I studied up on this."

"I never imagined — Well, what kind of roles do you think I'd fit?"

"All this time that we've been talking, I've been watching. Don't think I haven't. You remind me of someone. Let's see who it can be — one of the great oldtimers. Is it Milton Sills? No, that's not the one. Conway Tearle, Jack Mulhall? George Bancroft? No, his face was ruggeder. One thing I can tell you, though, a George Raft type you're not — those tough, smooth, black little characters."

"No, I wouldn't seem to be."

"No, you're not that flyweight type, with the fists from a nightclub, and the glamorous sideburns, doing the tango or the bolero. Not

Edward G. Robinson, either – I'm thinking aloud. Or the Cagney fly-in-your-face role, a cabbie, with that mouth and those punches.

"I realize that."

"Not suave like William Powell, or a lyric juvenile like Buddy Rogers. I suppose you don't play the sax? No. But –"

"But what?"

"I have you placed as the type that loses the girl to the George Raft type or the William Powell type. You are steady, faithful, you get stood up. The older women would know better. The mothers are on your side. With what they been through, if it was up to them, they'd take you in a minute. You're very sympathetic, even the young girls feel that. You'd make a good provider. But they go more for the other types. It's as clear as anything."

This was not how Wilhelm saw himself. And as he surveyed the old ground he recognized now that he had been not only confused but hurt. Why, he thought, he cast me even then for a loser.

Wilhelm had said, with half a mind to be defiant, "Is that your opinion?"

It never occurred to Venice that a man might object to stardom in such a role. "Here is your chance," he said. "Now you're just in college. What are you studying?" He snapped his fingers. "Stuff." Wilhelm himself felt this way about it. "You may plug along fifty years before you get anywheres. This way, in one jump, the world knows who you are. You become a name like Roosevelt, Swanson. From east to west, out to China, into South America. This is no bunk. You become a lover to the whole world. The world wants it, needs it. One fellow smiles, a billion people also smile. One fellow cries, the other billion sob with him. Listen, bud –" Venice had pulled himself together to make an effort. On his imagination there was some great weight which he could not discharge. He wanted Wilhelm, too, to feel it. He twisted his large, clean, well-meaning, rather foolish features as though he were their unwilling captive, and said in his choked, fat-obstructed voice, "Listen, everywhere there are people trying hard, miserable, in trouble, downcast, tired, trying and trying. They need a break, right? A break through, a help, luck or sympathy."

"That certainly is the truth," said Wilhelm. He had seized the feeling and he waited for Venice to go on. But Venice had no more to say; he had concluded. He gave Wilhelm several pages of blue hectographed script, stapled together, and told him to prepare for the screen test. "Study your lines in front of a mirror," he said. "Let yourself go. The part should take ahold of you. Don't be afraid to make faces and be emotional. Shoot the works. Because when you start to act you're no more an ordinary person, and those things don't apply to you. You don't behave the same way as the average."

And so Wilhelm had never returned to Penn State. His room-mate sent his things to New York for him, and the school authorities had to write to Dr Adler to find out what had happened.

Still for three months Wilhelm delayed his trip to California. He wanted to start out with the blessings of his family, but they were never given. He quarrelled with his parents and his sister. And then, when he was best aware of the risks and knew a hundred reasons against going and had made himself sick with fear, he left home. This was typical of Wilhelm. After much thought and hesitation and debate he invariably took the course he had rejected innumerable times. Ten such decisions made up the history of his life. He had decided that it would be a bad mistake to go to Hollywood, and then he went. He had made up his mind not to marry his wife, but ran off and got married. He had resolved not to invest money with Tamkin, and then had given him a cheque.

But Wilhelm had been eager for life to start. College was merely another delay. Venice had approached him and said that the world had named Wilhelm to shine before it. He was to be freed from the anxious and narrow life of the average. Moreover, Venice had claimed that he never made a mistake. His instinct for talent was infallible, he said.

But when Venice saw the results of the screen test he did a quick about-face. In those days Wilhelm had had a speech difficulty. It was not a true stammer, it was a thickness of speech which the sound track exaggerated. The film showed that he had many peculiarities, otherwise unnoticeable. When he shrugged, his hands drew up within his sleeves. The vault of his chest was huge, but he really didn't look strong under the lights. Though he called himself a hippopotamus, he more nearly resembled a bear. His walk was bear-like, quick and rather soft, toes turned inward, as though his shoes were an impediment. About one thing Venice had been right. Wilhelm was photogenic, and his wavy blond hair (now greying) came out well, but after the test Venice refused to encourage him. He tried to get rid of him. He couldn't afford to take a chance on him, he had made too many mistakes already and lived in fear of his powerful relatives.

Wilhelm had told his parents, "Venice says I owe it to myself to go." How ashamed he was now of this lie! He had begged Venice not to give him up. He had said, "Can't you help me out? It would kill me to go back to school now."

Then when he reached the Coast he learned that a recommendation from Maurice Venice was the kiss of death, Venice needed help and charity more than he, Wilhelm, ever had. A few years later when Wilhelm was down on his luck and working as an orderly in a Los Angeles hospital, he saw Venice's picture in the papers. He was under indictment for pandering. Closely following the trial, Wilhelm found out that Venice had indeed been employed by Kaskaskia Films but that he had evidently made use of the connexion to organize a ring of call-girls. Then what did he want with me? Wilhelm had cried to himself. He was unwilling to believe anything very bad about Venice. Perhaps he was foolish and unlucky, a fall guy, a dupe, a sucker. You didn't give a man fifteen years in prison for that. Wilhelm often thought that he might write him a letter to say how sorry he was. He remembered the breath of fate and Venice's certainty that he would be happy. 'Nita Christenberry was sentenced to three years. Wilhelm recognized her although she had changed her name.

By that time Wilhelm too had taken his new name. In California he became Tommy Wilhelm. Dr Adler would not accept the change. Today he still called his son Wilky, as he had done for more than forty years. Well, now, Wilhelm was thinking, the paper crowded in disarray under his arm, there's really very little that a man can change at will. He can't change his lungs, or nerves, or constitution or temperament. They're not under his control. When he's young and strong and impulsive and dissatisfied with the way things are he wants to rearrange them to assert his freedom. He can't overthrow the government or be differently born; he only has a little scope and maybe a foreboding, too, that essentially you can't change. Nevertheless, he makes a gesture and becomes Tommy Wilhelm. Wilhelm had always had a great longing to be Tommy. He had never, however, succeeded in feeling like Tommy, and in his soul had always remained Wilky. When he was drunk he reproached himself horribly as Wilky. "You fool, you clunk, you Wilky!" he called himself. He thought that it was a good thing perhaps that he had not become a success as Tommy since that would not have been a genuine success. Wilhelm would have feared that not he but Tommy had brought it off, cheating Wilky of his birthright. Yes, it had been a stupid thing to do, but it was his imperfect judgement at the age of twenty which should be blamed. He had cast off his father's name, and with it his father's opinion of him. It was, he knew it was, his bid for liberty. Adler being in his mind the title of the species. Tommy the freedom of the person. But Wilky was his inescapable self.

In middle age you no longer thought such thoughts about free choice. Then it came over you that from one grandfather you had inherited such and such a head of hair which looked like honey when it whitens or sugars in the jar; from another, broad thick shoulders; an oddity of speech from one uncle, and small teeth from another, and the grey eyes with darkness diffused even into the whites, and a wide-lipped mouth like a statue from Peru. Wandering races have such looks, the bones of one tribe, the skin of another. From his mother he had gotten sensitive feelings, a soft heart, a brooding nature, a tendency to be confused under pressure.

The changed name was a mistake, and he would admit it as freely as you liked. But this mistake couldn't be undone now, so why must his father continually remind him how he had sinned? It was too late. He would have to go back to the pathetic day when the sin was committed. And where was that day? Past and dead. Whose humiliating memories were these? His and not his father's. What had he to think back on that he could call good? Very, very little. You had to forgive. First, to forgive yourself, and then general forgiveness. Didn't he suffer from his mistakes far more than his father could?

"Oh, God," Wilhelm prayed. "Let me out of my trouble. Let me out of my thoughts, and let me do something better with myself. For all the time I have wasted I am very sorry. Let me out of this clutch and into a different life. For I am all balled up. Have mercy."

2

The mail.

The clerk who gave it to him did not care what sort of appearance he made this morning. He only glanced at him from under his brows, upward, as the letters changed hands. Why should the hotel people waste courtesies on him? They had his number. The clerk knew that he was handing him, along with the letters, a bill for his rent. Wilhelm assumed a look that removed him from all such things. But it was bad. To pay the bill he would have to withdraw money from his brokerage account, and the account was being watched because of the drop in lard. According to the *Tribune's* figures lard was still twenty points below last year's level. There were government price supports. Wilhelm didn't know how those worked but he understood that the farmer was protected and that the SEC kept an eye on the market and therefore he believed that lard would rise again and he wasn't greatly worried as yet. But in the meantime his father might have offered to pick up his hotel tab. Why didn't he? What a selfish old man he was! He saw his son's hardships; he could so easily help him. How little it would mean to him, and how much to Wilhelm! Where was the old man's heart? Maybe, thought Wilhelm, I was sentimental in the past and exaggerated his kindliness – warm family life. It may never have been there.

Not long ago his father had said to him in his usual affable, pleasant way, "Well, Wilky, here we are under the same roof again, after all these years."

Wilhelm was glad for an instant. At last they would talk over old times. But he was also on guard against insinuations. Wasn't his father saying, "Why are you here in a hotel with me and not at home in Brooklyn with your wife and two boys? You're neither a widower nor a bachelor. You have brought me all your confusions. What do you expect me to do with them?"

So Wilhelm studied the remark for a bit, then said, "The roof is twenty-six storeys up. But how many years has it been?"

"That's what I was asking you."

"Gosh, Dad, I'm not sure. Wasn't it the year Mother died? What year was that?"

He asked this question with an innocent frown on his Golden Grimes, dark blond face. *What year was it!* As though he didn't know the year, the month, the day, the very hour of his mother's death.

"Wasn't it nineteen-thirty-one?" said Dr Adler.

"Oh, was it?" said Wilhelm. And in hiding the sadness and the overwhelming irony of the question he gave a nervous shiver and wagged his head and felt the ends of his collar rapidly.

"Do you know?" his father said. "You must realize, an old fellow's memory becomes unreliable. It was in winter, that I'm sure of. Nineteen-thirty-two?"

Yes, it was age. Don't make an issue of it, Wilhelm advised himself. If you were to ask the old doctor in what year he had interned, he'd tell you correctly. All the same, don't make an issue. Don't quarrel with your own father. Have pity on an old man's failings.

"I believe the year was closer to nineteen-thirty-four, Dad," he said.

But Dr Adler was thinking. Why the devil can't he stand still when we're talking? He's either hoisting his pants up and down by the pockets or jittering with his feet. A regular mountain of tics, he's getting to be. Wilhelm had a habit of moving his feet back and forth as though, hurrying into a house, he had to clean his shoes first on the doormat.

Then Wilhelm had said, "Yes, that was the beginning of the end, wasn't it, Father?"

Wilhelm often astonished Dr Adler. Beginning of the end? What could he mean – what was he fishing for? Who's end? The end of family life? The old man was puzzled but he would not give Wilhelm an opening to introduce his complaints. He had learned that it was better not to take up Wilhelm's strange challenges. So he merely agreed pleasantly, for he was a master of social behaviour, and said, "It was an awful misfortune for us all."

He thought, What business has he to complain to *me* of his mother's death?

Face to face they had stood, each declaring himself silently after his own way. It was: it was not, the beginning of the end – *some* end.

Unaware of anything odd in his doing it, for he did it all the time, Wilhelm had pinched out the coal of his cigarette and dropped the butt in his pocket, where there were many more. And as he gazed at his father the little finger of his right hand began to twitch and tremble; of that he was unconscious, too.

And yet Wilhelm believed that when he put his mind to it he could have perfect and even distinguished manners, out-doing his father. Despite the slight thickness in his speech – it amounted almost to a stammer when he started the same phrase over several times in his effort to eliminate the thick sound – he could be fluent. Otherwise he would never have made a good salesman. He claimed also that he was a good listener. When he listened he made a tight mouth and rolled his eyes thoughtfully. He would soon tire and begin to utter short, loud, impatient breaths, and he would say, "Oh yes . . . yes . . . yes. I couldn't agree more." When he was forced to differ he would declare, "Well, I'm not sure. I don't really see it that way. I'm of two minds about it." He would never willingly hurt any man's feelings.

But in conversation with his father he was apt to lose control of himself. After any talk with Dr Adler, Wilhelm generally felt dissatisfied, and his dissatisfaction reached its greatest intensity when they discussed family matters. Ostensibly he had been trying to help the old man to remember a date, but in reality he meant to tell him, "You were set free when Ma died. You wanted to forget her. You'd like to get rid of Catherine, too. Me, too. You're not kidding anyone" – Wilhelm striving to put this across, and the old man not having it. In the end he was left struggling, while his father seemed unmoved.

And then once more Wilhelm had said to himself, "But, man! you're not a kid. Even then you weren't a kid!" He looked down over the front of his big, indecently big, spoiled body. He was beginning to lose his shape, his gut was fat, and he looked like a hippopotamus. His younger son called him "a hummuspotamus"; that was little Paul. And here he was still struggling with his old dad, filled with ancient grievances. Instead of saying, "Good-bye, youth! Oh, good-bye those marvellous, foolish wasted days. What a big clunk I was – I *am*."

Wilhelm was still paying heavily for his mistakes. His wife Margaret would not give him a divorce, and he had to support her and the two children. She would regularly agree to divorce him, and then think things over again and set new and more difficult conditions. No court would have awarded her the amounts he paid. One of today's letters, as he had expected, was from her. For the first time he had sent her a post-dated cheque, and she protested. She also enclosed bills for the boys' educational insurance policies, due next week. Wilhelm's mother-in-law had taken out these policies in Beverly Hills, and since her death two years ago he had to pay the premiums. Why couldn't she have minded her own business! They were his kids, and he took care of them and always would. He had planned to set up a trust fund. But that was on his former expectations. Now he had to rethink the future, because of the money problem. Meanwhile, here were the bills to be paid. When he saw the two sums punched out so neatly on the cards he cursed the company and its IBM equipment. His heart and his head were congested with anger. Everyone was supposed to have money. It was nothing to the company. It published pictures of funerals in the magazines and frightened the suckers, and then punched out little holes, and the customers would lie awake to think out ways to raise the dough. They'd be ashamed not to have it. They couldn't let a great company down, either, and they got the scratch. In the old days a man was put in prison for debt, but there were subtler things now. They made it a shame not to have money and set everybody to work.

Well, and what else had Margaret sent him? He tore the envelope open with his thumb, swearing that he would send any other bills back to her. There was, luckily, nothing more. He put the hole-punched cards in his pocket. Didn't Margaret know that he was nearly at the end of his rope? Of course. Her instinct told her that this was her opportunity, and she was giving him the works.

He went into the dining-room, which was under Austro-Hungarian management at the Hotel Gloriana. It was run like a European establishment. The pastries were excellent, especially the strudel. He often had apple strudel and coffee in the afternoon.

As soon as he entered he saw his father's small head in the sunny bay at the farther end, and heard his precise voice. It was with an odd sort of perilous expression that Wilhelm crossed the dining-room.

Dr Adler liked to sit in a corner that looked across Broadway down to the Hudson and New Jersey. On the other side of the street was a super-modern cafeteria with gold and purple mosaic columns. On the second floor a private-eye school, a dental laboratory, a reducing parlour, a veterans' club, and a Hebrew school shared the space. The old man was sprinkling sugar on his strawberries. Small hoops of brilliance were cast by the water glasses on the white tablecloth, despite a faint murkiness in the sunshine. It was early summer, and the long window was turned inward; a moth was on the pane; the putty was broken and the white enamel on the frames was streaming with wrinkles.

"Ha, Wilky," said the old man to his tardy son. "You haven't met our neighbour Mr Perls, have you? From the fifteenth floor."

"How d'do," Wilhelm said. He did not welcome this stranger; he began at once to find fault with him. Mr Perls carried a heavy cane with a crutch tip. Dyed hair, a skinny forehead – these were not reasons for bias. Nor was it Mr Perl's fault that Dr Adler was using him, not wishing to have breakfast with his son alone. But a gruffer voice within

Wilhelm spoke, asking, "Who is this damn frazzle-faced herring with his dyed hair and his fish teeth and this drippy moustache? Another one of Dad's German friends. Where does he collect all these guys? What is the stuff on his teeth? I never saw such pointed crowns. Are they stainless steel, or a kind of silver? How can a human face get into this condition. Uch!" Staring with his widely spaced grey eyes, Wilhelm sat, his broad back stooped under the sports jacket. He clasped his hands on the table with an implication of suppliance. Then he began to relent a little toward Mr Perls, beginning at the teeth. Each of those crowns represented a tooth ground to the quick, and estimating a man's grief with his teeth as two per cent of the total, and adding to that his flight from Germany and the probable origin of his wincing wrinkles, not to be confused with the wrinkles of his smile, it came to a sizeable load.

"Mr Perls was a hosiery wholesaler," said Dr Adler.

"Is this the son you told me was in the selling line?" said Mr Perls.

Dr Adler replied, "I have only this one son. One daughter. She was a medical technician before she got married – anaesthetist. At one time she had an important position in Mount Sinai."

He couldn't mention his children without boasting. In Wilhelm's opinion, there was little to boast of. Catherine, like Wilhelm, was big and fair-haired. She had married a court reporter who had a pretty hard time of it. She had taken a professional name, too – Philippa. At forty, she was still ambitious to become a painter. Wilhelm didn't venture to criticize her work. It didn't do much to him, he said, but then he was no critic. Anyway, he and his sister were generally on the outs and he didn't often see her paintings. She worked very hard, but there were fifty thousand people in New York with paints and brushes, each practically a law unto himself. It was the Tower of Babel in paint. *He* didn't want to go far into this. Things were chaotic all over.

Dr Adler thought that Wilhelm looked particularly untidy this morning – unrested, too, his eyes red-rimmed from excessive smoking. He was breathing through his mouth and he was evidently much distracted and rolled his red-shot eyes barbarously. As usual, his coat collar was turned up as though he had had to go out in the rain. When he went to business he pulled himself together a little; otherwise he let himself go and looked like hell.

"What's the matter, Wilky, didn't you sleep last night?"

"Not very much."

"You take too many pills of every kind – first stimulants and then depressants, anodynes followed by analeptics, until the poor organism doesn't know what's happened. Then the Luminal won't put people to sleep, and the Pervitin or Benzedrine won't wake them. God knows! These things get to be as serious as poisons, and yet everyone puts all their faith in them."

"No, Dad, it's not the pills. It's that I'm not used to New York any more. For a native, that's very peculiar, isn't it? It was never so noisy at night as now, and every little thing is a strain. Like the alternate parking. You have to run out at eight to move your car. And where can you put it? If you forget for a minute they tow you away. Then some fool puts advertising leaflets under your windshield wiper and you have heart failure a block away because you think you've got a ticket. When you do get stung with a ticket, you can't argue. You haven't got a chance in court and the city wants the revenue."

"But in your line you have to have a car, eh?" said Mr Perls.

"Lord knows why any lunatic would want one in the city who didn't need it for his livelihood."

Wilhelm's old Pontiac was parked in the street. Formerly, when on an expense account, he had always put it up in a garage. Now he was afraid to move the car from Riverside Drive lest he lose his space, and he used it only on Saturdays when the Dodgers were playing in Ebbets Field and he took his boys to the game. Last Saturday, when the Dodgers were out of town, he had gone out to visit his mother's grave.

Dr Adler had refused to go along. He couldn't bear his son's driving. Forgetfully, Wilhelm travelled for miles in second gear; he was seldom in the right lane and he neither gave signals nor watched for lights. The upholstery of his Pontiac was filthy with grease and ashes. One cigarette burned in the ash-tray, another in his hand, a third on the floor with maps and other waste paper and Coca-Cola bottles. He dreamed at the wheel or argued and gestured, and therefore the old doctor would not ride with him.

Then Wilhelm had come back from the cemetery angry because the stone bench between his mother's and his grandmother's graves had been overturned and broken by vandals. "Those damn teenage hoodlums get worse and worse," he said. "Why, they must have used a sledge-hammer to break the seat smack in half like that! If I could catch one of them!" He wanted the doctor to pay for a new seat, but his father was cool to the idea. He said he was going to have himself cremated.

Mr Perls said, "I don't blame you if you get no sleep up where you are." His voice was tuned somewhat sharp, as though he were slightly deaf. "Don't you have Parigi the singing teacher there? God, they have some queer elements in this hotel. On which floor is that Estonian woman with all her cats and dogs? They should have made her leave long ago."

"They've moved her down to twelve," said Dr Adler.

Wilhelm ordered a large Coca-Cola with his breakfast. Working in secret at the small envelopes in his pocket, he found two bills by touch. Much fingering had worn and weakened the paper. Under cover of a napkin he swallowed a Phenaphen sedative and a Unicap, but the doctor was sharp-eyed and said, "Wilky, what are you taking now?"

"Just my vitamin pills." He put his cigar butt in an ash-tray on the table behind him, for his father did not like the odour. Then he drank his Coca-Cola.

"That's what you drink for breakfast, and not orange juice?" said Mr Perls. He seemed to sense that he would not lose Dr Adler's favour by taking an ironic tone with his son.

"The caffeine stimulates brain activity," said the old doctor. "It does all kinds of things to the respiratory centre."

"It's just a habit of the road, that's all," Wilhelm said. "If you drive around long enough it turns your brains, your stomach, and everything else."

His father explained, "Wilky used to be with the Rojax Corporation. He was their north-eastern sales representative for a good many years but recently ended the connexion."

"Yes," said Wilhelm, "I was with them from the end of the war." He sipped the Coca-Cola and chewed the ice, glancing at one and the other with his attitude of large, shaky, patient dignity. The waitress set two boiled eggs before him.

"What kind of line does this Rojax company manufacture?" said Mr Perls.

"Kiddies' furniture. Little chairs, rockers, tables, Jungle-Gyms, slides, swings, seesaws."

Wilhelm let his father do the explaining. Large and stiff-backed, he tried to sit patiently, but his feet were abnormally restless. All right! His father had to impress Mr Perls? He would go along once more, and play his part. Fine! He would play along and help his father maintain his style. Style was the main consideration. That was just fine!

"I was with the Rojax Corporation for almost ten years," he said. "We parted ways because they wanted me to share my territory. They took a son-in-law into the business – new fellow. It was his idea."

To himself, Wilhelm said, Now God alone can tell why I have to lay my whole life bare to this blasted herring here. I'm sure nobody else does it. Other people keep their business to themselves. Not me.

He continued, "But the rationalization was that it was too big a territory for one man. I had a monopoly. That wasn't so. The real reason was that they had gotten to the place where they would have to make me an officer of the corporation. Vice presidency. I was in line for it, but instead this son-in-law got in, and –"

Dr Adler thought Wilhelm was discussing his grievances much too openly and said, "My son's income was up in the five figures."

As soon as money was mentioned, Mr Perls's voice grew eagerly sharper. "Yes? What, the thirty-two-per-cent bracket? Higher even, I guess?" He asked for a hint, and he named the figures not idly but with a sort of hugging relish. Uch! How they love money, thought Wilhelm. They adore money! Holy money! Beautiful money! It was getting so that people were feeble-minded about everything except money. While if you didn't have it you were a dummy, a dummy! You had to excuse yourself from the face of the earth. Chicken! That's what it was. The world's business. If only he could find a way out of it.

Such thinking brought on the usual congestion. It would grow into a fit of passion if he allowed it to continue. Therefore he stopped talking and began to eat.

Before he struck the egg with his spoon he dried the moisture with his napkin. Then he battered it (in his father's opinion) more than was necessary. A faint grime was left by his fingers on the white of the egg after he had picked away the shell. Dr Adler saw it with silent repugnance. What a Wilky he had given to the world! Why, he didn't even wash his hands in the morning. He used an electric razor so that he didn't have to touch water. The doctor couldn't bear Wilky's dirty habits. Only once – and never again, he swore – had he visited his room. Wilhelm, in pyjamas and stockings had sat on his bed, drinking gin from a coffee mug and rooting for the Dodgers on television. "That's two and two on you, Duke. Come on – hit it, now." He came down on the mattress – bam! The bed looked kicked to pieces. Then he drank the gin as though it were tea, and urged his team on with his fist. The smell of dirty clothes was outrageous. By the bedside lay a quart bottle and foolish magazines and mystery stories for the hours of insomnia. Wilhelm lived in worse filth than a savage. When the doctor spoke to him about this he answered, "Well, I have no wife to look after my things." And who – *who!* – had done the leaving? Not Margaret. The doctor was certain that she wanted him back.

Wilhelm drank his coffee with a trembling hand. In his full face his abused bloodshot grey eyes moved back and forth. Jerkily he set his cup back and put half the length of a cigarette into his mouth; he seemed to hold it with his teeth, as though it were a cigar.

"I can't let them get away with it," he said. "It's also a question of morale."

His father corrected him. "Don't you mean a moral question, Wilky?"

"I mean that, too. I have to do something to protect myself. I was promised executive standing." Correction before a stranger mortified him, and his dark blond face changed colour, more pale, and then more dark. He went on talking to Perls, but his eyes spied on his father. "I was the one who opened the territory for them. I could go back for one of their competitors and take away their customers. *My* customers. Morale enters into it because they've tried to take away my confidence."

"Would you offer a different line to the same people?" Mr Perls wondered.

"Why not? I know what's wrong with the Rojax product."

"Nonsense," said his father. "Just nonsense and kid's talk, Wilky. You're only looking for trouble and embarrassment that way. What would you gain by such a silly feud? You have to think about making a living and meeting your obligations."

Hot and bitter, Wilhelm said with pride, while his feet moved angrily under the table. "I don't have to be told about my obligations. I've been meeting them for years. In more than twenty years I've never had a penny of help from anybody. I preferred to dig a ditch on the WPA but never asked anyone to meet my obligations for me."

"Wilky has had all kinds of experiences," said Dr Adler.

The old doctor's face had a wholesome reddish and almost translucent colour, like a ripe apricot. The wrinkles beside his ears were deep because the skin conformed so tightly to his bones. With all his might, he was a healthy and fine small old man. He wore a white vest of a light check pattern. His hearing-aid doodad was in the pocket. An unusual shirt of red and black stripes covered his chest. He bought his clothes in a college shop farther uptown. Wilhelm thought he had no business to get himself up like a jockey, out of respect for his profession.

"Well," said Mr Perls. "I can understand how you feel. You want to fight it out. By a certain time of life, to have to start all over again can't be a pleasure, though a good man can always do it. But anyway you want to keep on with a business you know already, and not have to meet a whole lot of new contacts."

Wilhelm again thought, Why does it have to be me and my that's discussed, and not him and his life? He would never allow it. But I am an idiot. I have no reserve. To me it can be done. I talk. I must ask for it. Everybody wants to have intimate conversations, but the smart fellows don't give out, only the fools. The smart fellows talk intimately about the fools, and examine them all over and give them advice. Why do I allow it? The hint about his age had hurt him. No, you can't admit it's as good as ever, he conceded. Things do give out.

"In the meanwhile," Dr Adler said, "Wilky is taking it easy and considering various propositions. Isn't that so?"

"More or less," said Wilhelm. He suffered his father to increase Mr Perls's respect for him. The WPA ditch had brought the family into contempt. He was a little tired. The spirit, the peculiar burden of his existence lay upon him like an accretion, a load, a hump. In any moment of quiet, when sheer fatigue prevented him from struggling, he was apt to feel this mysterious weight, this growth or collection of nameless things which it was the business of his life to carry about. That must be what a man was for. This large, odd, excited, fleshy, blond, abrupt personality named Wilhelm, or Tommy, was here, present, in the present – Dr Tamkin had been putting into his mind many suggestions about the present moment, the here and now – this Wilky, or Tommy Wilhelm, forty-four years old, father of two sons, at present living in the Hotel Gloriana, was assigned to be the carrier of a load which was his own self, his characteristic self. There was no figure or estimate for the value of this load. But it is probably exaggerated by the subject, T. W. Who is a visionary sort of animal. Who has to believe that he can know why he exists. Though he has never seriously tried to find out why.

Mr Perls said, "If he wants time to think things over and have a rest, why doesn't he run down to Florida for a while? Off season it's cheap and quiet. Fairy-land. The mangoes are just coming in. I got two acres down there. You'd think you were in India."

Mr Perls utterly astonished Wilhelm when he spoke of fairyland with a foreign accent. Mangoes – India? What did he mean, India?

"Once upon a time," said Wilhelm, "I did some public relations work for a big hotel down in Cuba. If I could get them a notice in Leonard Lyons or one of the other columns it might be good for another holiday there, gratis. I haven't had a vacation for a long time, and I could stand a rest after going so hard. You know that's true, Father." He meant that his father knew how deep the crisis was becoming; how badly he was strapped for money; and that he could not rest but would be crushed if he stumbled; and that his obligations would destroy him. He couldn't falter. He thought, The money! When I had it, I flowed money. They bled it away from me. I haemorrhaged money. But now it's almost all gone, and where am I supposed to turn for more?

He said, "As a matter of fact, Father, I am tired as hell."

But Mr Perls began to smile and said, "I understand from Doctor Tamkin that you're going into some kind of investment with him, partners."

"You know, he's a very ingenious fellow," said Dr Adler. "I really enjoy hearing him go on. I wonder if he really is a medical doctor."

"Isn't he?" said Perls. "Everybody thinks he is. He talks about his patients. Doesn't he write prescriptions?"

"I don't really know what he does," said Dr Adler. "He's a cunning man."

"He's a psychologist, I understand," said Wilhelm.

"I don't know what sort of psychologist or psychiatrist he may be," said his father. "He's a little vague. It's growing into a major industry, and a very expensive one. Fellows have to hold down very big jobs in order to pay those fees. Anyway, this Tamkin is clever. He never said he practised here, but I believe he was a doctor in California. They don't seem to have much legislation out there to cover these things, and I hear a thousand dollars will get you a degree from a Los Angeles correspondence school. He gives the impression of knowing something about chemistry, and things like hypnotism. I wouldn't trust him, though."

"And why wouldn't you?" Wilhelm demanded.

"Because he's probably a liar. Do you believe he invented all the things he claims?"

Mr Perls was grinning.

"He was written up in *Fortune*," said Wilhelm. "Yes, in *Fortune* magazine. He showed me the article. I've seen his clippings."

"That doesn't make him legitimate," said Dr Adler. "It might have been another Tamkin. Make no mistake, he's an operator. Perhaps even crazy."

"Crazy, you say?"

Mr Perls put in, "He could be both sane and crazy. In these days nobody can tell for sure which is which."

"An electrical device for truck drivers to wear in their caps," said Dr Adler, describing one of Tamkin's proposed inventions. "To wake them with a shock when they begin to be drowsy at the wheel. It's triggered by the change in blood-pressure when they start to doze."

"It doesn't sound like such an impossible thing to me," said Wilhelm.

Mr Perls said, "To me he described an underwater suit so a man could walk on the bed of the Hudson in case of an atomic attack. He said he could walk to Albany in it."

"Ha, ha, ha, ha, ha!" cried Dr Adler in his old man's voice. "Tamkin's Folly. You could go on a camping trip under Niagara Falls."

"This is just his kind of fantasy," said Wilhelm. "It doesn't mean a thing. Inventors are supposed to be like that. I get funny ideas myself. Everybody wants to make something. Any American does."

But his father ignored this and said to Perls, "What other inventions did he describe?"

While the frazzle-faced Mr Perls and his father in the unseemly, monkey-striped shirt were laughing, Wilhelm could not restrain himself and joined in with his own panting laugh. But he was in despair. They were laughing at the man to whom he had given a power of attorney over his last seven hundred dollars to speculate for him in the commodities markets. They had bought all that lard. It had to rise today. By ten o'clock, or half past ten, trading would be active, and he would see.

Between white tablecloths and glassware and glancing silverware, through overfull light, the long figure of Mr Perls went away into the darkness of the lobby. He thrust with his cane, and dragged a large built-up shoe which Wilhelm had not included in his estimate of troubles. Dr Adler wanted to talk about him. "There's a poor man," he said, "with a bone condition which is gradually breaking him up."

"One of those progressive diseases?" said Wilhelm.

"Very bad. I've learned," the doctor told him, "to keep my sympathy for the real ailments. This Perls is more to be pitied than any man I know."

Wilhelm understood he was being put on notice and did not express his opinion. He ate and ate. He did not hurry but kept putting food on his plate until he had gone through the muffins and his father's strawberries, and then some pieces of bacon that were left; he had several cups of coffee, and when he was finished he sat gigantically in a state of arrest and didn't seem to know what he should do next.

For a while father and son were uncommonly still. Wilhelm's preparations to please Dr Adler had failed completely, for the old man kept thinking, You'd never guess he had a clean upbringing, and, What a dirty devil this son of mine is. Why can't he try to sweeten his appearance a little? Why does he want to drag himself like this? And he makes himself look so idealistic.

Wilhelm sat, mountainous. He was not really so slovenly as his father found him to be. In some aspects he even had a certain delicacy. His mouth, though broad, had a fine outline, and his brow and his gradually incurved nose, dignity, and in his blond hair there was white but there were also shades of gold and chestnut. When he was with the Rojax Corporation Wilhelm had kept a small apartment in Roxbury, two rooms in a large house with a small porch and garden, and on mornings of leisure, in late spring weather like this, he used to sit expanded in a wicker chair with the sunlight pouring through the weave, and sunlight through the slug-eaten holes of the young hollyhocks and as deeply as the grass allowed into small flowers. This peace (he forgot that that time had had its troubles, too), this peace was gone. It must not have belonged to him, really, for to be here in New York with his old father was more genuinely like his life. He was well aware that he didn't stand a chance of getting sympathy from his father, who said he kept his for real ailments. Moreover, he advised himself repeatedly not to discuss his vexatious problems with him, for his father, with some justice, wanted to be left in peace. Wilhelm also knew that when he began to talk about these things he made himself feel worse, he became congested with them and worked himself into a clutch. Therefore he warned himself, Lay off, pal. It'll only be an aggravation. From a deeper source, however, came other promptings. If he didn't keep his troubles before him he risked losing them altogether, and he knew by experience that this was worse. And furthermore, he could not succeed in excusing his father on the ground of old age. No. No, he could not. I am his son, he thought. He is my father. He is as much father as I am son – old or not. Affirming this, though in complete silence, he sat, and, sitting, he kept his father at the table with him.

"Wilky," said the old man, "have you gone down to the baths here yet?"

"No, Dad, not yet."

"Well, you know the Gloriana has one of the finest pools in New York. Eighty feet, blue tile. It's a beauty."

Wilhelm had seen it. On the way to the gin game you passed the stairway to the pool. He did not care for the odour of the wall-locked and chlorinated water.

"You ought to investigate the Russian and Turkish baths, and the sunlamps and massage. I don't hold with sunlamps. But the masssage does a world of good, and there's nothing better than hydrotherapy when you come right down to it. Simple water has a calming effect and would do you more good than all the barbiturates and alcohol in the world."

Wilhelm reflected that this advice was as far as his father's help and sympathy would extend.

"I thought," he said, "that the water cure was for lunatics."

The doctor received this as one of his son's jokes and said with a smile, "Well, it won't turn a sane man into a lunatic. It does a great deal for me. I couldn't live without my massages and steam."

"You're probably right. I ought to try it one of these days. Yesterday, late in the afternoon, my head was about to bust and I just had to have a little air, so I walked around the reservoir, and I sat down for a while in a playground. It rests me to watch the kids play potsy and skiprope."

36

The doctor said with approval, "Well, now, that's more like the idea."

"It's the end of the lilacs," said Wilhelm. "When they burn it's the beginning of the summer. At least, in the city. Around the time of year when the candy stores take down the windows and start to sell sodas on the sidewalk. But even though I was raised here, Dad, I can't take city life any more, and I miss the country. There's too much push here for me. It works me up too much. I take things too hard. I wonder why you never retired to a quieter place."

The doctor opened his small hand on the table in a gesture so old and so typical that Wilhelm felt it like an actual touch upon the foundations of his life. "I am a city boy myself, you must remember," Dr Adler explained. "But if you find the city so hard on you, you ought to get out."

"I'll do that," said Wilhelm, "as soon as I can make the right connexion. Meanwhile –"

His father interrupted, "Meanwhile I suggest you cut down on drugs."

"You exaggerate that, Dad. I don't really – I give myself a little boost against –" He almost pronounced the word "misery" but he kept his resolution not to complain.

The doctor, however, fell into the error of pushing his advice too hard. It was all he had to give his son and he gave it once more. "Water and exercise," he said.

He wants a young, smart, successful son, thought Wilhelm, and he said, "Oh, Father, it's nice of you to give me this medical advice, but steam isn't going to cure what ails me."

The doctor measurably drew back, warned by the sudden weak strain of Wilhelm's voice and all that the droop of his face, the swell of his belly against the restraint of his belt intimated.

"Some new business?" he asked unwillingly.

Wilhelm made a great preliminary summary which involved the whole of his body. He drew and held a long breath, and his colour changed and his eyes swam. "New?" he said.

"You make too much of your problems," said the doctor. "They ought not to be turned into a career. Concentrate on real troubles – fatal sickness, accidents." The old man's whole manner said, Wilky, don't start this on me. I have a right to be spared.

Wilhelm himself prayed for restraint; he knew this weakness of his and fought it. He knew, also, his father's character. And he began mildly, "As far as the fatal part of it goes, everyone on this side of the grave is the same distance from death. No, I guess my trouble is not exactly new. I've got to pay premiums on two policies for the boys. Margaret sent them to me. She unloads everything on me. Her mother left her an income. She won't even file a joint tax return. I get stuck. Etcetera. But you've heard the whole story before."

"I certainly have," said the old man. "And I've told you to stop giving her so much money."

Wilhelm worked his lips in silence before he could speak. The congestion was growing. "Oh, but my kids, Father. My kids. I love them. I don't want them to lack anything."

The doctor said with a half-deaf benevolence, "Well, naturally. And she, I'll bet, is the beneficiary of that policy."

"Let her be. I'd sooner die myself before I collected a cent of such money."

"Ah yes." The old man sighed. He did not like the mention of death. "Did I tell you that your sister Catherine – Philippa – is after me again."

"What for?"

"She wants to rent a gallery for an exhibition."

Stiffly fair-minded, Wilhelm said, "Well, of course that's up to you, Father."

The round-headed old man with his fine, feather-white, ferny hair said, "No, Wilky. There's not a thing on those canvases. I don't believe it; it's a case of the emperor's clothes. I may be old enough for my second childhood, but at least the first is well behind me. I was glad enough to buy crayons for her when she was four. But now she's a woman of forty and too old to be encouraged in her delusions. She's no painter."

"I wouldn't go so far as to call her a born artist," said Wilhelm, "but you can't blame her for trying something worth while."

"Let her husband pamper her."

Wilhelm had done his best to be just to his sister, and he had sincerely meant to spare his father, but the old man's tight, benevolent deafness had its usual effect on him. He said, "When it comes to women and money, I'm completely in the dark. What makes Margaret act like this?"

"She's showing you that you can't make it without her," said the doctor. "She aims to bring you back by financial force."

"But if she ruins me, Dad, how can she expect me to come back? No, I have a sense of honour. What you don't see is that she's trying to put an end to me."

His father stared. To him this was absurd. And Wilhelm thought, Once a guy starts to slip, he figures he might as well be a clunk. A real big clunk. He even takes pride in it. But there's nothing to be proud of – hey, boy? Nothing. I don't blame Dad for his attitude. And it's no cause for pride.

"I don't understand that. But if you feel like this why don't you settle with her once and for all?"

"What do you mean, Dad?" said Wilhelm, surprised. "I thought I told you. Do you think I'm not willing to settle? Four years ago when we broke up I gave her everything – goods, furniture, savings. I tried to show good will – but I didn't get anywhere. Why, when I wanted Scissors, the dog, because the animal and I were so attached to each other – it was bad enough to leave the kids – she absolutely refused me. Not that she cared a damn about the animal. I don't think you've seen him. He's an Australian sheep dog. They usually have one blank or whitish eye which gives a misleading look, but they're the gentlest dogs and have unusual delicacy about eating or talking. Let me at least have the companionship of this animal. Never." Wilhelm was greatly moved. He wiped his face at all corners with his napkin. Dr Adler felt that his son was indulging himself too much in his emotions.

"Whenever she can hit me, she hits, and she seems to live for that alone. And she demands more and more, and still more. Two years ago she wanted to go back to college and get another degree. It increased my burden but I thought it would be wiser in the end if she got a better job through it. But still she takes as much from me as before. Next thing she'll want to be a Doctor of Philosophy. She says the women in her family live long, and I'll have to pay and pay for the rest of my life."

The doctor said impatiently, "Well, these are details, not principles. Just details which you can leave out. The dog! You're mixing up all kinds of irrelevant things. Go to a good lawyer."

"But I've already told you, Dad. I got a lawyer, and she got one, too, and both of them talk and send me bills, and I eat my heart out. Oh, Dad, Dad, what a hole I'm in!" said Wilhelm in utter misery. "The lawyers –

see? – draw up an agreement, and she says okay on Monday and wants more money on Tuesday. And it begins again."

"I always thought she was a strange kind of woman," said Dr Adler. He felt that by disliking Margaret from the first and disapproving of the marriage he had done all that he could be expected to do.

"Strange, Father! I'll show you what she's like." Wilhelm took hold of his broad throat with brown-stained fingers and bitten nails and began to choke himself.

"What are you doing?" cried the old man.

"I'm showing you what she does to me."

"Stop that – stop it!" the old man said and tapped the table commandingly.

"Well, Dad, she hates me. I feel that she's strangling me. I can't catch my breath. She just has fixed herself on me to kill me. She can do it at long distance. One of these days I'll be struck down by suffocation or apoplexy because of her. I just can't catch my breath."

"Take your hands off your throat, you foolish man," said his father. "Stop this bunk. Don't expect me to believe in all kinds of voodoo."

"If that's what you want to call it, all right." His face flamed and paled and swelled and his breath was laborious.

"But I'm telling you that from the time I met her I've been a slave. The Emancipation Proclamation was only for coloured people. A husband like me is a slave, with an iron collar. The churches go up to Albany and supervise the law. They won't have divorces. The court says, "You want to be free. Then you have to work twice as hard – twice, at least! Work! you bum." So then guys kill each other for the buck, and they may be free of a wife who hates them but they are sold to the company. The company knows a guy has got to have his salary, and takes full advantage of him. Don't talk to me about being free. A rich man may be free on an income of a million net. A poor man may be free because nobody cares what he does. But a fellow in my position has to sweat it out until he drops dead."

His father replied to this, "Wilky, it's entirely your own fault. You don't have to allow it."

Stopped in his eloquence, Wilhelm could not speak for a while. Dumb and incompetent, he struggled for breath and frowned with effort into his father's face.

"I don't understand your problems," said the old man. "I never had any like them."

By now Wilhelm had lost his head and he waved his hands and said over and over, "Oh, Dad, don't give me that stuff, don't give me that. Please don't give me that sort of thing." 5

"It's true," said his father. "I come from a different world. Your mother and I led an entirely different life."

"Oh, how can you compare Mother," Wilhelm said. "Mother was a help to you. Did she harm you ever?"

"There's no need to carry on like an opera, Wilky," said the doctor. 10 "This is only your side of things."

"What? It's the truth," said Wilhelm.

The old man could not be persuaded and shook his round head and drew his vest down over the gilded shirt, and leaned back with a completeness of style that made this look, to anyone out of hearing, like 15 an ordinary conversation between a middle-aged man and his respected father. Wilhelm towered and swayed, big and sloven, with his grey eyes red-shot and his honey-coloured hair twisted in flaming shapes upward. Injustice made him angry, made him beg. But he wanted an understanding with his father, and he tried to capitulate to him. He said, "You can't 20 compare Mother and Margaret, and neither can you and I be compared, because you, Dad, were a success. And a success – is a success. I never made a success."

The doctor's old face lost all of its composure and became hard and angry. His small breast rose sharply under the red and black shirt and he 25 said, "Yes. Because of hard work. I was not self-indulgent, not lazy. My old man sold dry goods in Williamsburg. We were nothing, do you understand? I knew I couldn't afford to waste my chances."

"I wouldn't admit for one minute that I was lazy," said Wilhelm. "If anything, I tried too hard. I admit I made many mistakes. Like I thought 30 I shouldn't do things you had done already. Study chemistry. You had done it already. It was in the family."

His father continued, "I didn't run around with fifty women, either. I was not a Hollywood star. I didn't have time to go to Cuba for a vacation. I stayed at home and took care of my children." 35

Oh, thought Wilhelm, eyes turning upward. Why did I come here in the first place, to live near him? New York is like a gas. The colours are running. My head feels so tight, I don't know what I'm doing. He thinks

I want to take away his money or that I envy him. He doesn't see what I want.

"Dad," Wilhelm said aloud, "you're being very unfair. It's true the movies was a false step. But I love my boys. I didn't abandon them. I left Margaret because I had to."

"Why did you have to?"

"Well –" said Wilhelm, struggling to condense his many reasons into a few plain words. "I had to – I had to."

With sudden and surprising bluntness his father said, "Did you have bed-trouble with her? Then you should have stuck it out. Sooner or later everyone has it. Normal people stay with it. It passes. But you wouldn't, so now you pay for your stupid romantic notions. Have I made my view clear?"

It was very clear. Wilhelm seemed to hear it repeated from various sides and inclined his head different ways, and listened and thought. Finally he said, "I guess that's the medical standpoint. You may be right. I just couldn't live with Margaret. I wanted to stick it out, but I was getting very sick. She was one way and I was another. She wouldn't be like me, so I tried to be like her, and I couldn't do it."

"Are you sure she didn't tell *you* to go?" the doctor said.

"I wish she had. I'd be in a better position now. No, it was me. I didn't want to leave, but I couldn't stay. Somebody had to take the initiative. I did. Now I'm the fall guy too."

Pushing aside in advance all the objections that his son would make, the doctor said, "Why did you lose your job with Rojax?"

"I didn't, I've told you."

"You're lying. You wouldn't have ended the connexion. You need the money too badly. But you must have got into trouble." The small old man spoke concisely and with great strength. "Since you have to talk and can't let it alone, tell the truth. Was there a scandal – a woman?"

Wilhelm fiercely defended himself. "No, Dad, there wasn't any woman. I told you how it was."

"Maybe it was a man, then," the old man said wickedly.

Shocked, Wilhelm stared at him with burning pallor and dry lips. His skin looked a little yellow. "I don't think you know what you're talking about," he answered after a moment. "You shouldn't let your imagination run so free. Since you've been living here on Broadway you

42

must think you understand life, up to date. You ought to know your own son a little better. Let's drop that, now."

"All right, Wilky, I'll withdraw it. But something must have happened in Roxbury nevertheless. You'll never go back. You're just talking wildly about representing a rival company. You won't. You've done something to spoil your reputation, I think. But you've got girl friends who are expecting you back, isn't that so?"

"I take a lady out now and then while on the road," said Wilhelm. "I'm not a monk."

"No one special? Are you sure you haven't gotten into complications?"

He had tried to unburden himself and instead, Wilhelm thought, he had to undergo an inquisition to prove himself worthy of a sympathetic word. Because his father believed that he did all kinds of gross things.

"There is a woman in Roxbury that I went with. We fell in love and wanted to marry, but she got tired of waiting for my divorce. Margaret figured that. On top of which the girl was a Catholic and I had to go with her to the priest and make an explanation."

Neither did this last confession touch Dr Adler's sympathies or sway his calm old head or affect the colour of his complexion.

"No, no, no, no; all wrong," he said.

Again Wilhelm cautioned himself. Remember his age. He is no longer the same person. He can't bear trouble. I'm so choked up and congested anyway I can't see straight. Will I ever get out of the woods, and recover my balance? You're never the same afterward. Trouble rusts out the system.

"You really *want* a divorce?" said the old man.

"For the price I pay I should be getting something."

"In that case," Dr Adler said, "it seems to me no normal person would stand for such treatment from a woman."

"Ah, Father, Father!" said Wilhelm. "It's always the same thing with you. Look how you lead me on. You always start out to help me with my problems, and be sympathetic and so forth. It gets my hopes up and I begin to be grateful. But before we're through I'm a hundred times more depressed than before. Why is that? You have no sympathy. You want to shift all the blame on to me. Maybe you're wise to do it." Wilhelm was beginning to lose himself. "All you seem to think about is your death. Well, I'm sorry. But I'm going to die too. And I'm your son.

It isn't my fault in the first place. There ought to be a right way to do this, and be fair to each other. But what I want to know is, why do you start up with me if you're not going to help me? What do you want to know about my problems for, Father? So you can lay the whole responsibility on me – so that you won't have to help me? D'you want me to comfort you for having such a son?" Wilhelm had a great knot of wrong tied tight within his chest, and tears approached his eyes but he didn't let them out. He looked shabby enough as it was. His voice was thick and hazy, and he was stammering and could not bring his awful feelings forth.

"You have some purpose of your own," said the doctor, "in acting so unreasonable. What do you want from me? What do you expect?"

"What do I expect?" said Wilhelm. He felt as though he were unable to recover something. Like a ball in the surf, washed beyond reach, his self-control was going out. "I expect *help*!" The words escaped him in a loud, wild, frantic cry and startled the old man, and two or three breakfasters within hearing glanced their way. Wilhelm's hair, the colour of whitened honey, rose dense and tall with the expansion of his face, and he said, "When I suffer – you aren't even sorry. That's because you have no affection for me, and you don't want any part of me."

"Why must I like the way you behave? No, I don't like it," said Dr Adler.

"All right. You want me to change myself. But suppose I could do it – what would I become? What could I? Let's suppose that all my life I have had the wrong ideas about myself and wasn't what I thought I was. And wasn't even careful to take a few precautions, as most people do – like a woodchuck has a few exits to his tunnel. But what shall I do now? More than half my life is over. More than half. And now you tell me I'm not even normal."

The old man too had lost his calm. "You cry about being helped," he said. "When you thought you had to go into the service I sent a cheque to Margaret every month. As a family man you could have had an exemption. But no! The war couldn't be fought without you and you had to get yourself drafted and be an office-boy in the Pacific theatre. Any clerk could have done what you did. You could find nothing better to become than a GI."

Wilhelm was going to reply, and half raised his bearish figure from the chair, his fingers spread and whitened by their grip on the table, but the old man would not let him begin. He said, "I see other elderly people here with children who aren't much good, and they keep backing them and holding them up at a great sacrifice. But I'm not going to make that mistake. It doesn't enter your mind that when I die – a year, two years from now – you'll still be here. I do think of it."   5

He had intended to say that he had a right to be left in peace. Instead he gave Wilhelm the impression that he meant it was not fair for the better man of the two and the more useful, the more admired, to leave the world first. Perhaps he meant that, too – a little; but he would not under other circumstances have come out with it so flatly.   10

"Father," said Wilhelm with an unusual openness of appeal. "Don't you think I know how you feel? I have pity. I want you to live on and on. If you outlive me, that's perfectly okay by me." As his father did not answer this avowal and turned away his glance, Wilhelm suddenly burst out, "No, but you hate me. And if I had money you wouldn't. By God,   15
you have to admit it. The money makes the difference. Then we would be a fine father and son, if I was a credit to you – so you could boast and brag about me all over the hotel. But I'm not the right type of son. I'm too old, I'm too old and too unlucky."

His father said, "I can't give you any money. There would be no end   20
to it if I started. You and your sister would take every last buck from me. I'm still alive, not dead. I am still here. Life isn't over yet. I am as much alive as you or anyone. And I want nobody on my back. Get off! And I give you the same advice, Wilky. Carry nobody on your back."

"Just keep your money," said Wilhelm miserably. "Keep it and enjoy   25
it yourself. That's the ticket!"

4

Ass! Idiot! Wild boar! Dumb mule! Slave! Lousy, wallowing hippopotamus! Wilhelm called himself as his bending legs carried him from the dining-room. His pride! His inflamed feelings! His begging   30
and feebleness! And trading insults with his old father – and spreading confusion over everything. Oh, how poor, contemptible, and ridiculous he was! When he remembered how he had said, with great reproof, 'You ought to know your own son' – why, how corny and abominable it was.
                                                                          35

He could not get out of the sharply brilliant dining-room fast enough. He was horribly worked up; his neck and shoulders, his entire chest ached as though they had been tightly tied with ropes. He smelled the salt odour of tears in his nose.

But at the same time, since there were depths in Wilhelm not unsuspected by himself, he received a suggestion from some remote element in his thoughts that the business of life, the real business – to carry his peculiar burden, to feel shame and impotence, to taste these quelled tears – the only important business, the highest business was being done. Maybe the making of mistakes expressed the very purpose of his life and the essence of his being here. Maybe he was supposed to make them and suffer from them on this earth. And though he had raised himself above Mr Perls and his father because they adored money, still they were called to act energetically and this was better than to yell and cry, pray and beg, poke and blunder and go by fits and starts and fall upon the thorns of life. And finally sink beneath that watery floor – would that be tough luck, or would it be good riddance?

But he raged once more against his father. Other people with money, while they're still alive, want to see it do some good. Granted, he shouldn't support me. But have I ever asked him to do that? Have I ever asked for dough at all, either for Margaret or for the kids or for myself? It isn't the money, but only the assistance; not even assistance, but just the feeling. But he may be trying to teach me that a grown man should be cured of such feeling. Feeling got me in dutch at Rojax. I had the *feeling* that I belonged to the firm, and my *feelings* were hurt when they put Gerber in over me. Dad thinks I'm too simple. But I'm not so simple as he thinks. What about his feelings? He doesn't forget death for one single second, and that's what makes him like this. And not only is death on his mind but through money he forces me to think about it, too. It gives him power over me. He forces me that way, he himself, and then he's sore. If he was poor, I could care for him and show it. The way I *could* care, too, if I only had a chance. He'd see how much love and respect I had in me. It would make him a different man, too. He'd put his hands on me and give me his blessing.

Someone in a grey straw hat with a wide cocoa-coloured band spoke to Wilhelm in the lobby. The light was dusky, splotched with red underfoot; green, the leather furniture; yellow, the indirect lighting.

"Hey, Tommy. Say, there."

46

"Excuse me," said Wilhelm, trying to reach a house phone. But this was Dr Tamkin, whom he was just about to call.

"You have a very obsessional look on your face," said Dr Tamkin.

Wilhelm thought, Here he is, here he is. If I could only figure this guy out.

"Oh," he said to Tamkin. "Have I got such a look? Well, whatever it is, you name it and I'm sure to have it."

The sight of Dr Tamkin brought his quarrel with his father to a close. He found himself flowing into another channel.

"What are we doing?" he said. "What's going to happen to lard today?"

"Don't worry yourself about that. All we have to do is hold on to it and it's sure to go up. But what's made you so hot under the collar, Wilhelm?"

"Oh, one of those family situations." This was the moment to take a new look at Tamkin, and he viewed him closely but gained nothing by the new effort. It was conceivable that Tamkin was everything that he claimed to be, and all the gossip false. But was he a scientific man, or not? If he was not, this might be a case for the district attorney's office to investigate. Was he a liar? That was a delicate question. Even a liar might be trustworthy in some ways. Could he trust Tamkin – could he? He feverishly, fruitlessly sought an answer.

But the time for this question was past, and he had to trust him now. After a long struggle to come to a decision, he had given him the money. Practical judgement was in abeyance. He had worn himself out, and the decision was no decision. How had this happened? But how had his Hollywood career begun? It was not because of Maurice Venice, who turned out to be a pimp. It was because Wilhelm himself was ripe for the mistake. His marriage, too, had been like that. Through such decisions somehow his life had taken form. And so, from the moment when he tasted the peculiar flavour of fatality in Dr Tamkin, he could no longer keep back the money.

Five days ago Tamkin had said, "Meet me tomorrow, and we'll go to the market." Wilhelm, therefore, had had to go. At eleven o'clock they had walked to the brokerage office. On the way, Tamkin broke the news to Wilhelm that though this was an equal partnership he couldn't put up his half of the money just yet; it was tied up for a week or so in one of his patents. Today he would be two hundred dollars short; next week, he'd

47

make it up. But neither of them needed an income from the market, of course. This was only a sporting proposition anyhow, Tamkin said. Wilhelm had to answer, "Of course." It was too late to withdraw. What else could he do? Then came the formal part of the transaction, and it was frightening. The very shade of green of Tamkin's cheque looked wrong; it was a false, disheartening colour. His handwriting was peculiar, even monstrous; the e's were like i's, the t's and I's the same, and the h's like wasps' bellies. He wrote like a fourth-grader. Scientists, however, dealt mostly in symbols; they printed. This was Wilhelm's explanation.

Dr Tamkin had given him his cheque for three hundred dollars. Wilhelm, in a blinded and convulsed aberration, pressed and pressed to try to kill the trembling of his hand as he wrote out his cheque for a thousand. He set his lips tight, crouched with his huge back over the table, and wrote with crumbling, terrified fingers, knowing that if Tamkin's cheque bounced his own would not be honoured either. His sole cleverness was to set the date ahead by one day to give the green cheque time to clear.

Next he had signed a power of attorney, allowing Tamkin to speculate with his money, and this was an even more frightening document. Tamkin had never said a word about it, but here they were and it had to be done.

After delivering his signatures, the only precaution Wilhelm took was to come back to the manager of the brokerage office and ask him privately, "Uh, about Doctor Tamkin. We were in here a few minutes ago, remember?"

That day had been a weeping, smoky one and Wilhelm had gotten away from Tamkin on the pretext of having to run to the post office. Tamkin had gone to lunch alone, and here was Wilhelm, back again, breathless, his hat dripping, needlessly asking the manager if he remembered.

"Yes, sir, I know," the manager had said. He was a cold, mild, lean German who dressed correctly and around his neck wore a pair of opera glasses with which he read the board. He was an extremely correct person except that he never shaved in the morning, not caring, probably, how he looked to the fumblers and the old people and the operators and the gamblers and the idlers of Broadway uptown. The market closed at three. Maybe, Wilhelm guessed, he had a thick beard and took a lady out to dinner later and wanted to look fresh-shaven.

"Just a question," said Wilhelm. "A few minutes ago I signed a power of attorney so Doctor Tamkin could invest for me. You gave me the blanks."

"Yes, sir, I remember." 5

"Now this is what I want to know," Wilhelm had said. "I'm no lawyer and I only gave the paper a glance. Does this give Doctor Tamkin power of attorney over any other assets of mine – money, or property?"

The rain had dribbled from Wilhelm's deformed, transparent 10 raincoat; the buttons of his shirt, which always seemed tiny, were partly broken, in pearly quarters of the moon, and some of the dark, thick golden hairs that grew on his belly stood out. It was the manager's business to conceal his opinion of him; he was shrewd, grey, correct (although unshaven) and had little to say except on matters that came to 15 his desk. He must have recognized in Wilhelm a man who reflected long and then made the decision he had rejected twenty separate times. Silvery, cool, level, long-profiled, experienced, indifferent, observant, with unshaven refinement, he scarcely looked at Wilhelm, who trembled with fearful awkwardness. The manager's face, low-coloured, 20 long-nostrilled, acted as a unit of perception; his eyes merely did their reduced share. Here was a man, like Rubin, who knew and knew. He, a foreigner, knew; Wilhelm, in the city of his birth, was ignorant.

The manager had said, "No, sir, it does not give him."

"Only over the funds I deposited with you?" 25

"Yes, that is right, sir."

"Thank you, that's what I wanted to find out," Wilhelm had said, grateful.

The answer comforted him. However, the question had no value. None at all. For Wilhelm had no other assets. He had given Tamkin his 30 last money. There wasn't enough of it to cover his obligations anyway, and Wilhelm had reckoned that he might as well go bankrupt now as next month. "Either broke or rich," was how he had figured, and that formula had encouraged him to make the gamble. Well, not rich; he did not expect that, but perhaps Tamkin might really show him how to earn 35 what he needed in the market. By now, however, he had forgotten his own reckoning and was aware only that he stood to lose his seven hundred dollars to the last cent.

Dr Tamkin took the attitude that they were a pair of gentlemen experimenting with lard and grain futures. The money, a few hundred dollars, meant nothing much to either of them. He said to Wilhelm, "Watch. You'll get a big kick out of this and wonder why more people don't go into it. You think the Wall Street guys are so smart – geniuses? That's because most of us are psychologically afraid to think about the details. Tell me this. When you're on the road, and you don't understand what goes on under the hood of your car, you'll worry what'll happen if something goes wrong with the engine. Am I wrong?" No, he was right. "Well," said Dr Tamkin with an expression of quiet triumph about his mouth, almost the suggestion of a jeer. "It's the same psychological principle, Wilhelm. They are rich because you don't understand what goes on. But it's no mystery, and by putting in a little money and applying certain principles of observation, you begin to grasp it. It can't be studied in the abstract. You have to take a specimen risk so that you feel the process, the money-flow, the whole complex. To know how it feels to be a seaweed you have to get in the water. In a very short time we'll take out a hundred-per-cent profit." Thus Wilhelm had had to pretend at the outset that his interest in the market was theoretical.

"Well," said Tamkin when he met him now in the lobby, "what's the problem, what is this family situation? Tell me." He put himself forward as the keen mental scientist. Whenever this happened Wilhelm didn't know what to reply. No matter what he said or did it seemed that Dr Tamkin saw through him.

"I had some words with my dad."

Dr Tamkin found nothing extraordinary in this. "It's the eternal same story," he said. "The elemental conflict of parent and child. It won't end, ever. Even with a fine old gentleman like your dad."

"I don't suppose it will. I've never been able to get anywhere with him. He objects to my feelings. He thinks they're sordid. I upset him and he gets mad at me. But maybe all old men are alike."

"Sons, too. Take it from one of them," said Dr Tamkin. "All the same, you should be proud of such a fine old patriarch of a father. It should give you hope. The longer he lives, the longer your life-expectancy becomes."

Wilhelm answered, brooding, "I guess so. But I think I inherit more from my mother's side, and she died in her fifties."

"A problem arose between a young fellow I'm treating and his dad – I just had a consultation," said Dr Tamkin as he removed his dark grey hat.

"So early in the morning?" said Wilhelm with suspicion.

"Over the telephone, of course."

What a creature Tamkin was when he took off his hat! The indirect light showed the many complexities of his bald skull, his gull's nose, his rather handsome eyebrows, his vain moustache, his deceiver's brown eyes. His figure was stocky, rigid, short in the neck, so that the large ball of the occiput touched his collar. His bones were peculiarly formed, as though twisted twice where the ordinary human bone was turned only once, and his shoulders rose in two pagoda-like points. At mid-body he was thick. He stood pigeon-toed, a sign perhaps that he was devious or had much to hide. The skin of his hands was ageing, and his nails were moonless, concave, clawlike, and they appeared loose. His eyes were as brown as beaver fur and full of strange lines. The two large brown naked balls looked thoughtful – but were they? And honest – but was Dr Tamkin honest? There was a hypnotic power in his eyes, but this was not always of the same strength, nor was Wilhelm convinced that it was completely natural. He felt that Tamkin tried to make his eyes deliberately conspicuous, with studied art, and that he brought forth his hypnotic effect by an exertion. Occasionally it failed or drooped, and when this happened the sense of his face passed downward to his heavy (possibly foolish?) red underlip.

Wilhelm wanted to talk about the lard holdings, but Dr Tamkin said, "This father-and-son case of mine would be instructive to you. It's a different psychological type completely than your dad. This man's father thinks that he isn't his son."

"Why not?"

"Because he has found out something about the mother carrying on with a friend of the family for twenty-five years."

"Well, what do you know!" said Wilhelm. His silent thought was, Pure bull. Nothing but bull!

"You must note how interesting the woman is, too. She has two husbands. Whose are the kids? The fellow detected her and she gave a signed confession that two of the four children were not the father's."

"It's amazing," said Wilhelm, but he said it in a rather distant way. He was always hearing such stories from Dr Tamkin. If you were to believe

Tamkin, most of the world was like this. Everybody in the hotel had a mental disorder, a secret history, a concealed disease. The wife of Rubin at the news-stand was supposed to be kept by Carl, the yelling, loud-mouthed gin-rummy player. The wife of Frank in the barbershop had disappeared with a GI while he was waiting for her to disembark at the French Lines pier. Everyone was like the faces on a playing card, upside down either way. Every public figure had a character-neurosis. Maddest of all were the businessmen, the heartless, flaunting, boisterous business class who ruled this country with their hard manners and their bold lies and their absurd words that nobody could believe. They were crazier than anyone. They spread the plague. Wilhelm, thinking of the Rojax Corporation, was inclined to agree that many businessmen were insane. And he supposed that Tamkin, for all his peculiarities, spoke a kind of truth and did some people a sort of good. It confirmed Wilhelm's suspicions to hear that there was a plague, and he said, "I couldn't agree with you more. They trade on anything, they steal everything, they're cynical right to the bones."

"You have to realize," said Tamkin, speaking of his patient, or his client, "that the mother's confession isn't good. It's a confession of duress. I try to tell the young fellow he shouldn't worry about a phony confession. But what does it help him if I am rational with him?"

"No?" said Wilhelm, intensely nervous. "I think we ought to go over to the market. It'll be opening soon."

"Oh, come on," said Tamkin. "It isn't even nine o'clock, and there isn't much trading the first hour anyway. Things don't get hot in Chicago until half past ten, and they're an hour behind us, don't forget. Anyway, I say lard will go up, and it will. Take my word. I've made a study of the guilt-aggression cycle which is behind it. I ought to know *something* about that. Straighten your collar."

"But meantime," said Wilhelm, "we have taken a licking this week. Are you sure your insight is at its best? Maybe when it isn't we should lay off and wait."

"Don't you realize," Dr Tamkin told him, "you can't march in a straight line to the victory? You fluctuate toward it. From Euclid to Newton there were straight lines. The modern age analyses the wavers. On my own accounts, I took a licking in hides and coffee. But I have confidence I'm sure I'll out-guess them." He gave Wilhelm a narrow smile, friendly, calming, shrewd, and wizard-like, patronizing, secret, potent. He saw his fears and smiled at them. "It's something," he remarked, "to see how the competition factor will manifest itself in different individuals."

"So? Let's go over."

"But I haven't had my breakfast yet."

"I've had mine."

"Come, have a cup of coffee."

"I wouldn't want to meet my dad." Looking through the glass doors, Wilhelm saw that his father had left by the other exit. Wilhelm thought, He didn't want to run into me, either. He said to Dr Tamkin, "Okay, I'll sit with you, but let's hurry it up because I'd like to get to the market while there's still a place to sit. Everybody and his uncle gets in ahead of you."

"I want to tell you about this boy and his dad. It's highly absorbing. The father was a nudist. Everybody went naked in the house. Maybe the woman found men *with* clothes attractive. Her husband didn't believe in cutting his hair, either. He practised dentistry. In his office he wore riding pants and a pair of boots, and he wore a green eyeshade."

"Oh, come off it," said Wilhelm.

"This is a true case history."

Without warning, Wilhelm began to laugh. He himself had had no premonition of his change of humour. His face became warm and pleasant, and he forgot his father, his anxieties; he panted bearlike, happily, through his teèth. "This sounds like a horse-dentist. He wouldn't have to put on pants to treat a horse. Now what else are you going to tell me? Did the wife play the mandolin? Does the boy join the cavalry? Oh, Tamkin, you really are a killer-diller."

"Oh, you think I'm trying to amuse you," said Tamkin. "That's because you aren't familiar with my outlook. I deal in facts. Facts always are sensational. I'll say that a second time. Facts *always!* are sensational."

Wilhelm was reluctant to part with his good mood. The doctor had little sense of humour. He was looking at him earnestly.

"I'd bet you any amount of money," said Tamkin, "that the facts about you are sensational."

"Oh – ha, ha! You want them? You can sell them to a true confession magazine."

"People forget how sensational the things are that they do. They don't see it in themselves. It blends into the background of their daily life."

Wilhelm smiled. "Are you sure this boy tells the truth?"

"Yes, because I've known the whole family for years."

"And you do psychological work with your own friends? I didn't know that was allowed."

"Well, I'm a radical in the profession. I have to do good wherever I can."

Wilhelm's face became ponderous again and pale. His whitened gold hair lay heavy on his head, and he clasped uneasy fingers on the table. Sensational, but oddly enough, dull, too. Now how do you figure that out? It blends with the background. Funny but unfunny. True but false. Casual but laborious, Tamkin was. Wilhelm was most suspicious of him when he took his driest tone.

"With me," said Dr Tamkin, "I am at my most efficient when I don't need the fee. When I only love. Without a financial reward. I remove myself from the social influence. Especially money. The spiritual compensation is what I look for. Bringing people into the here-and-now. The real universe. That's the present moment. The past is no good to us. The future is full of anxiety. Only the present is real – the here-and-now. Seize the day."

"Well," said Wilhelm, his earnestness returning. "I know you are a very unusual man. I like what you say about here-and-now. Are all the people who come to see you personal friends and patients too? Like that tall handsome girl, the one who always wears those beautiful broomstick skirts and belts?"

"She was an epileptic, and a most bad and serious pathology, too. I'm curing her successfully. She hasn't had a seizure in six months, and she used to have one every week."

"And that young cameraman, the one who showed us those movies from the jungles of Brazil, isn't he related to her?"

"Her brother. He's under my care, too. He has some terrible tendencies, which are to be expected when you have an epileptic sibling. I came into their lives when they needed help desperately, and took hold of them. A certain man forty years older than she had her in his control and used to give her fits by suggestion whenever she tried to leave him. If you only knew one per cent of what goes on in the city of New York! You see, I understand what it is when the lonely person begins to feel like an animal. When the night comes and he feels like howling from his window like a wolf. I'm taking complete care of that young fellow and his sister. I have to steady him down or he'll go from Brazil to Australia the next day. The way I keep him in the here-and-now is by teaching him Greek."

This was a complete surprise! "What, do you know Greek?"

"A friend of mine taught me when I was in Cairo. I studied Aristotle with him to keep from being idle."

Wilhelm tried to take in these new claims and examine them. Howling from the window like a wolf when night comes sounded genuine to him. That was something really to think about. But the Greek! He realized that Tamkin was watching to see how he took it. More elements were continually being added. A few days ago Tamkin had hinted that he had once been in the underworld, one of the Detroit Purple Gang. He was once head of a mental clinic in Toledo. He had worked with a Polish inventor on an unsinkable ship. He was a technical consultant in the field of television. In the life of a man of genius, all of these things might happen. But had they happened to Tamkin? Was he a genius? He often said that he had attended some of the Egyptian royal family as a psychiatrist. "But everybody is alike, common or aristocrat," he told Wilhelm. "The aristocrats knows less about life."

An Egyptian princess whom he had treated in California, for horrible disorders he had described to Wilhelm, retained him to come back to the old country with her, and there he had had many of her friends and relatives under his care. They turned over a villa on the Nile to him. "For ethical reasons, I can't tell you many of the details about them," he said – but Wilhelm had already heard all these details, and strange and shocking they were, if true. *If* true – he could not be free from doubt. For instance, the general who had to wear ladies' silk stockings and stand otherwise naked before the mirror – and all the rest. Listening to the doctor when he was so strangely factual. Wilhelm had to translate his words into his own language, and he could not translate fast enough or find terms to fit what he heard.

"Those Egyptian big shots invested in the market, too, for the heck of it. What did they need extra money for? By association, I almost became a millionaire myself, and if I had played it smart there's no telling what might have happened. I could have been the ambassador." The American? The Egyptian ambassador? "A friend of mine tipped

me off on the cotton. I made a heavy purchase of it. I didn't have that kind of money, but everybody there knew me. It never entered their minds that a person of their social circle didn't have dough. The sale was made on the phone. Then, while the cotton shipment was at sea, the
5 price tripled. When the stuff suddenly became so valuable all hell broke loose on the world cotton market, they looked to see who was the owner of this big shipment. Me! They investigated my credit and found out I was a mere doctor, and they cancelled. This was illegal. I sued them. But as I didn't have the money to fight them I sold the suit to a Wall Street
10 lawyer for twenty thousand dollars. He fought it and was winning. They settled with him out of court for more than a million. But on the way back from Cairo, flying, there was a crash. All on board died. I have this guilt on my conscience, of being the murderer of that lawyer. Although he was a crook."

15 Wilhelm thought, I must be a real jerk to sit and listen to such impossible stories. I guess I am a sucker for people who talk about the deeper things of life, even the way he does.

"We scientific men speak of irrational guilt, Wilhelm," said Dr Tamkin, as if Wilhelm were a pupil in his class. "But in such a situation,
20 because of the money, I wished him harm. I realize it. This isn't the time to describe all the details, but the money made me guilty. *M*oney and *M*urder both begin with *M*. *M*achinery. *M*ischief."

Wilhelm, his mind thinking for him at random, said, "What about *M*ercy? *M*ilk-of-human-kindness?"

25 "One fact should be clear to you by now. Money-making is aggression. That's the whole thing. The functionalistic explanation is the only one. People come to the market to kill. They say, 'I'm going to make a killing.' It's not accidental. Only they haven't got the genuine courage to kill, and they erect a symbol of it. The money. They make a
30 killing by a fantasy. Now, counting the number is always a sadistic activity. Like hitting. In the Bible, the Jews wouldn't allow you to count them. They knew it was sadistic."

"I don't understand what you mean," said Wilhelm. A strange uneasiness tore at him. The day was growing too warm and his head felt
35 dim. "What makes them want to kill?"

"By and by you'll get the drift," Dr Tamkin assured him. His amazing eyes had some of the rich dryness of a brown fur. Innumerable crystalline hairs or spicules of light glittered in their bold

56

surfaces. "You can't understand without first spending years on the study of the ultimates of human and animal behaviour, the deep chemical, organismic, and spiritual secrets of life. I am a psychological poet."

"If you're this kind of poet," said Wilhelm, whose fingers in his pocket were feeling in the little envelopes for the Phenaphen capsules, "what are you doing on the market?"

"That's a good question. Maybe I am better at speculation because I don't care. Basically, I don't wish hard enough for money, and therefore I come with a cool head to it."

Wilhelm thought, Oh, sure! That's an answer, is it? I bet that if I took a strong attitude he'd back down on everything. He'd grovel in front of me. The way he looks at me on the sly, to see if I'm being taken in! He swallowed his Phenaphen pill with a long gulp of water. The rims of his eyes grew red as it went down. And then he felt calmer.

"Let me see if I can give you an answer that will satisfy you," said Dr Tamkin. His flapjacks were set before him. He spread the butter on them, poured on brown maple syrup, quartered them, and began to eat with hard, active, muscular jaws which sometimes gave a creak at the hinges. He pressed the handle of his knife against his chest and said, "In here, the human bosom – mine, yours, everybody's – there isn't just one soul. There's a lot of souls. But there are two main ones, the real soul and a pretender soul. Now! Every man realizes that he has to love something or somebody. He feels that he must go outward. 'If thou canst not love, what art thou?' Are you with me?"

"Yes, Doc, I think so," said Wilhelm listening – a little sceptically but none the less hard.

" 'What art thou?' Nothing. That's the answer. Nothing. In the heart of hearts – Nothing! So of course you can't stand that and want to be Something, and you try. But instead of being this Something, the man puts it over on everybody instead. You can't be that strict to yourself. You love a *little*. Like you have a dog" (*Scissors!*) "or give some money to a charity drive. Now that isn't love, is it? What is it? Egotism, pure and simple. It's a way to love the pretender soul. Vanity. Only vanity, is what it is. And social control. The interest of the pretender soul is the same as the interest of the social life, the society mechanism. This is the main tragedy of human life. Oh, it is terrible! Terrible! You are not free. Your own betrayer is inside of you and sells you out. You have to obey him like a slave. He makes you work like a horse. And for what? For who?"

"Yes, for what?" The doctor's words caught Wilhelm's heart. "I couldn't agree more," he said. "When do we get free?"

"The purpose is to keep the whole thing going. The true soul is the one that pays the price. It suffers and gets sick, and it realizes that the pretender can't be loved. Because the pretender is a lie. The true soul loves the truth. And when the true soul feels like this, it wants to kill the pretender. The love has turned into hate. Then you become dangerous. A killer. You have to kill the deceiver."

"Does this happen to everybody?"

The doctor answered simply, "Yes, to everybody. Of course, for simplification purposes, I have spoken of the soul; it isn't a scientific term, but it helps you to understand it. Whenever the slayer slays, he wants to slay the soul in him which was gypped and deceived him. Who is his enemy? Him. And his lover? Also. Therefore, all suicide is murder, and all murder is suicide. It's the one and identical phenomenon. Biologically, the pretender soul takes away the energy of the true soul and makes it feeble, like a parasite. It happens unconsciously, unawaringly, in the depths of the organism. Ever take up parasitology?"

"No, it's my dad who's the doctor."

"You should read a book about it."

Wilhelm said, "But this means that the world is full of murderers. So it's not the world. It's a kind of hell."

"Sure," the doctor said. "At least a kind of purgatory. You walk on the bodies. They are all around. I can hear them cry *de profundis* and wring their hands. I hear them, poor human beasts. I can't help hearing. And my eyes are open to it. I have to cry, too. This is the human tragedy-comedy."

Wilhelm tried to capture his vision. And again the doctor looked untrustworthy to him, and he doubted him. "Well," he said, "there are also kind, ordinary, helpful people. They're – out in the country. All over. What kind of morbid stuff do you read, anyway?" The doctor's room was full of books.

"I read the best of literature, science and philosophy," Dr Tamkin said. Wilhelm had observed that in his room even the TV aerial was set upon a pile of volumes. "Korzybski, Aristotle, Freud, W. H. Sheldon, and all the great poets. You answer me like a layman. You haven't applied your mind strictly to this."

"Very interesting," said Wilhelm. He was aware that he hadn't applied his mind strictly to anything. "You don't have to think I'm a dummy, though. I have ideas too." A glance at the clock told him that the market would soon open. They could spare a few minutes yet. There were still more things he wanted to hear from Tamkin. He realized that Tamkin spoke faultily, but then scientific men were not always strictly literate. It was the description of the two souls that had awed him. In Tommy he saw the pretender. And even Wilky might not be himself. Might the name of his true soul be the one by which his old grandfather had called him – Velvel? The name of a soul, however, must be only that – soul. What did it look like? Does my soul look like me? Is there a soul that looks like Dad? Like Tamkin? Where does the true soul get its strength? Why does it have to love truth? Wilhelm was tormented, but tried to be oblivious to his torment. Secretly, he prayed the doctor would give him some useful advice and transform his life. "Yes, I understand you," he said. "It isn't lost on me."

"I never said you weren't intelligent, but only you just haven't made a study of it all. As a matter of fact you're a profound personality with very profound creative capacities but also disturbances. I've been concerned with you, and for some time I've been treating you."

"Without my knowing it? I haven't felt you doing anything. What do you mean? I don't think I like being treated without my knowledge. I'm of two minds. What's the matter, don't you think I'm normal?" And he really was divided in mind. That the doctor cared about him pleased him. This was what he craved, that someone should care about him, wish him well. Kindness, mercy, he wanted. But – and here he retracted his heavy shoulders in his peculiar way, drawing his hands up into his sleeves; his feet moved uneasily under the table – but he was worried, too, and even somewhat indignant. For what right had Tamkin to meddle without being asked? What kind of privileged life did this man lead? He took other people's money and speculated with it. Everybody came under his care. No one could have secrets from him.

The doctor looked at him with his deadly brown, heavy, impenetrable eyes, his naked shining head, his red hanging underlip, and said, "You have lots of guilt in you."

Wilhelm helplessly admitted, as he felt the heat rise to his wide face,

"Yes, I think so, too. But personally," he added, "I don't feel like a murderer. I always try to lay off. It's the others who get me. You know – make me feel oppressed. And if you don't mind, and it's all the same to you, I would rather know it when you start to treat me. And now, Tamkin, for Christ's sake, they're putting out the lunch menus already. Will you sign the check, and let's go!"

Tamkin did as he asked, and they rose. They were passing the book-keeper's desk when he took out a substantial bundle of onion-skin papers and said, "These are receipts of the transactions. Duplicates. You'd better keep them as the account is in your name and you'll need them for income taxes. And here is a copy of a poem I wrote yesterday."

"I have to leave something at the desk for my father," Wilhelm said, and he put his hotel bill in an envelope with a note. *Dear Dad, Please carry me this month. Yours, W.* He watched the clerk with his sullen pug's profile and his stiff-necked look push the envelope into his father's box.

"May I ask you really why you and your dad had words?" said Dr Tamkin, who had hung back, waiting.

"It was about my future," said Wilhelm. He hurried down the stairs with swift steps, like a tower in motion, his hands in his trousers pockets. He was ashamed to discuss the matter. "He says there's a reason why I can't go back to my old territory, and there is. I told everybody I was going to be an officer of the corporation. And I was supposed to. It was promised. But then they welshed because of the son-in-law. I bragged and made myself look big."

"If you was humble enough, you could go back. But it doesn't make much difference. We'll make you a good living on the market."

They came into the sunshine of upper Broadway, not clear but throbbing through the dust and fumes, a false air of gas visible at eye-level as it spurted from the bursting buses. From old habit, Wilhelm turned up the collar of his jacket.

"Just a technical question," Wilhelm said. "What happens if your losses are bigger than your deposit?"

"Don't worry. They have ultra-modern electronic book-keeping machinery, and it won't let you get in debt. It puts you out automatically. But I want you to read this poem. You haven't read it yet."

Light as a locust, a helicopter bringing mail from Newark Airport to La Guardia sprang over the city in a long leap.

The paper Wilhelm unfolded had ruled borders in red ink. He read:

Mechanism vs Functionalism
Ism vs Hism

If thee thyself couldst only see
Thy greatness that is and yet to be,   5
Thou would feel joy-beauty-what ecstasy.
They are at thy feet, earth-moon-sea, the trinity.

Why-forth then dost thou tarry
And partake thee only of the crust
And skim the earth's surface narry   10
When all creations art thy just?

Seek ye then that which art not there
In thine own glory let thyself rest.
Witness. Thy power is not bare.
Thou art King. Thou art at thy best.   15

Look then right before thee.
Open thine eyes and see.
At the foot of Mt Serenity
Is thy cradle to eternity.

Utterly confused, Wilhelm said to himself explosively, What kind of   20
mishmash, claptrap is this! What does he want from me? Damn him to
hell, he might as well hit me on the head, and lay me out, kill me. What
does he give me this for? What's the purpose? Is it a deliberate test?
Does he want to mix me up? He's already got me mixed up completely. I
was never good at riddles. Kiss those seven hundred bucks good-bye,   25
and call it one more mistake in a long line of mistakes – Oh, Mama, what
a line! He stood near the shining window of a fancy fruit store, holding
Tamkin's paper, rather dazed, as though a charge of photographer's
flash powder had gone up in his eyes.

But he's waiting for my reaction. I have to say something to him   30
about his poem. It really is no joke. What will I tell him? Who is this
King? The poem is written *to* someone. But who? I can't even bring
myself to talk. I feel too choked and strangled. With all the books he
reads, how come the guy is so illiterate? And why do people just
naturally assume that you'll know what they're talking about? No, I   35

don't know, and nobody knows. The planets don't, the stars don't, infinite space doesn't. It doesn't square with Planck's Constant or anything else. So what's the good of it? Where's the need of it? What does he mean here by Mount Serenity? Could it be a figure of speech for Mount Everest? As he says people are all committing suicide, maybe those guys who climbed Everest were only trying to kill themselves, and if we want peace we should stay at the foot of the mountain. In the here-and-now. But it's also here-and-now on the slope, and on the top, where they climbed to seize the day. Surface narry is something he can't mean, I don't believe. I'm about to start foaming at the mouth. "Thy cradle . . ." *Who* is resting in his cradle – in his glory? My thoughts are at an end. I feel the wall. No more. So –k it all! The money and everything. Take it away! When I have the money they eat me alive, like those piranha fish in the movie about the Brazilian jungle. It was hideous when they ate up that Brahma bull in the river. He turned pale, just like clay, and in five minutes nothing was left except the skeleton still in one piece, floating away. When I haven't got it any more, at least they'll let me alone.

"Well, what do you think of this?" said Dr Tamkin. He gave a special sort of wise smile, as though Wilhelm must now see what kind of man he was dealing with.

"Nice. Very nice. Have you been writing long?"

"I've been developing this line of thought for years and years. You follow it all the way?"

"I'm trying to figure out who this Thou is."

"Thou? Thou is you."

"Me! Why? This applies to *me*?"

"Why shouldn't it apply to you. You were in my mind when I composed it. Of course, the hero of the poem is sick humanity. If it would open its eyes it would be great."

"Yes, but how do I get into this?"

"The main idea of the poem is *con*struct or *de*struct. There is no ground in between. Mechanism is *de*struct. Money of course is *de*struct. When the last grave is dug, the gravedigger will have to be paid. If you could have confidence in nature you would not have to fear. It would keep you up. Creative is nature. Rapid. Lavish. Inspirational. It shapes leaves. It rolls the waters of the earth. Man is the chief of this. All creations are his just inheritance. You don't know what you've got

within you. A person either creates or he destroys. There is no neutrality
. . ."

"I realized you were no beginner," said Wilhelm with propriety. "I
have only one criticism to make. I think 'whyforth' is wrong. You
should write, 'Wherefore then dost thou . . .'" And he reflected, So? I
took a gamble. It'll have to be a miracle, though, to save me. My money
will be gone, then it won't be able to destruct me. He can't just take and
lose it, though. He's in it, too. I think he's in a bad way himself. He must
be. I'm sure because, come to think of it, he sweated blood when he
signed that cheque. But what have I let myself in for? The waters of the
earth are going to roll over me.

∫

Patiently, in the window of the fruit store, a man with a scoop spread
crushed ice between his rows of vegetables. There were also Persian
melons, lilacs, tulips with radiant black at the middle. The many street
noises came back after a little while from the caves of the sky. Crossing
the tide of Broadway traffic, Wilhelm was saying to himself, The reason
Tamkin lectures me is that somebody has lectured him, and the reason
for the poem is that he wants to give me good advice. Everybody seems
to know something. Even fellows like Tamkin. Many people know
what to do, but how many can do it?

He believed that he must, that the could and would recover the good
things, the happy things, the easy tranquil things of life. He had made
mistakes, but he could overlook these. He had been a fool, but that
could be forgiven. The time wasted – must be relinquished. What else
could one do about it? Things were too complex, but they might be
reduced to simplicity again. Recovery was possible. First he had to get
out of the city. No, first he had to pull out his money . . .

From the carnival of the street – pushcarts, accordion and fiddle,
shoeshine, begging, the dust going round like a woman on stilts – they
entered the narrow crowded theatre of the brokerage office. From front
to back it was filled with the Broadway crowd. But how was lard doing
this morning? From the rear of the hall Wilhelm tried to read the tiny
figures. The German manager was looking through his binoculars.

63

Tamkin placed himself on Wilhelm's left and covered his conspicuous bald head. "The guy'll ask me about the margin," he muttered. They passed, however, unobserved. "Look, the lard has held its place," he said.

Tamkin's eyes must be very sharp to read the figures over so many heads and at this distance – another respect in which he was unusual.

The room was always crowded. Everyone talked. Only at the front could you hear the flutter of the wheels within the board. Teletyped news items crossed the illuminated screen above.

"Lard. Now what about rye?" said Tamkin, rising on his toes. Here he was a different man, active and impatient. He parted people who stood in his way. His face turned resolute, and on either side of his mouth odd bulges formed under his moustache. Already he was pointing out to Wilhelm the appearance of a new pattern on the board. "There's something up today," he said.

"Then why'd you take so long with breakfast?" said Wilhelm.

There were no reserved seats in the room, only customary ones. Tamkin always sat in the second row, on the commodities side of the aisle. Some of his acquaintances kept their hats on the chairs for him.

"Thanks. Thanks," said Tamkin, and he told Wilhelm, " I fixed it up yesterday."

"That was a smart thought," said Wilhelm. They sat down.

With folded hands, by the wall, sat an old Chinese businessman in a seersucker coat. Smooth and fat, he wore a white Vandyke. One day Wilhelm had seen him on Riverside Drive pushing two little girls along in a baby carriage – his grandchildren. Then there were two women in their fifties, supposed to be sisters, shrewd and able money-makers, according to Tamkin. They had never a word to say to Wilhelm. But they would chat with Tamkin. Tamkin talked to everyone.

Wilhelm sat between Mr Rowland, who was elderly, and Mr Rappaport, who was very old. Yesterday Rowland had told him that in the year 1908, when he was a junior at Harvard, his mother had given him twenty shares of steel for his birthday, and then he had started to read the financial news and had never practised law but instead followed the market for the rest of his life. Now he speculated only in soy beans, of which he had made a speciality. By his conservative method, said Tamkin, he cleared two hundred a week. Small potatoes, but then he was a bachelor, retired, and didn't need money.

"Without dependants," said Tamkin. "He doesn't have the problems that you and I do."

Did Tamkin have dependants? He had everything that it was possible for a man to have — science, Greek, chemistry, poetry, and now dependants too. That beautiful girl with epilepsy, perhaps. He often said that she was a pure, marvellous, spiritual child who had no knowledge of the world. He protected her, and, if he was not lying, adored her. And if you encouraged Tamkin by believing him, or even if you refrained from questioning him, his hints became more daring. Sometimes he said that he paid for her music lessons. Sometimes he seemed to have footed the bill for the brother's camera expedition to Brazil. And he spoke of paying for the support of the orphaned child of a dead sweetheart. These hints, made dully as asides, grew by repetition into sensational claims.

"For myself, I don't need much," said Tamkin. "But a man can't live for himself and I need the money for certain important things. What do you figure you have to have, to get by?"

"Not less than fifteen grand, after taxes. That's for my wife and the two boys."

"Isn't there anybody else?" said Tamkin with a shrewdness almost cruel. But his look grew more sympathetic as Wilhelm stumbled, not willing to recall another grief.

"Well — there was. But it wasn't a money matter."

"I should hope!" said Tamkin. "If love is love, it's free. Fifteen grand, though, isn't too much for a man of your intelligence to ask out of life. Fools, hard-hearted criminals, and murderers have millions to squander. They burn up the world — oil, coal, wood, metal, and soil, and suck even the air and the sky. They consume, and they give back no benefit. A man like you, humble for life, who wants to feel and live, has trouble — not wanting," said Tamkin in his parenthetical fashion, "to exchange an ounce of soul for a pound of social power — he'll never make it without help in a world like this. But don't you worry." Wilhelm grasped at this assurance. "Just you never mind. We'll go easily beyond your figure."

Dr Tamkin gave Wilhelm comfort. He often said that he had made as much as a thousand a week in commodities. Wilhelm had examined the receipts, but until this moment it had never occurred to him that there must be debit slips too; he had been shown only the credits.

"But fifteen grand is not an ambitious figure," Tamkin was telling him. "For that you don't have to wear yourself out on the road, dealing with narrow-minded people. A lot of them don't like Jews, either, I suppose?"

"I can't afford to notice. I'm lucky when I have my occupation. Tamkin, do you mean you can save our money?"

"Oh, did I forget to mention what I did before closing yesterday? You see, I closed out one of the lard contracts and bought a hedge of December rye. The rye is up three points already and takes some of the sting out. But lard will go up, too."

"Where? God, yes, you're right," said Wilhelm, eager, and got to his feet to look. New hope freshened his heart. "Why didn't you tell me before?"

And Tamkin, smiling like a benevolent magician, said, "You must learn to have trust. The slump in lard can't last. And just take a look at eggs. Didn't I predict they couldn't go any lower? They're rising and rising. If we had taken eggs we'd be far ahead."

"Then why didn't we take them?"

"We were just about to. I had a buying order in at .24, but the tide turned at .26^1/$_4$ and we barely missed. Never mind. Lard will go back to last year's levels."

Maybe. But when? Wilhelm could not allow his hopes to grow too strong. However, for a little while he could breathe more easily. Late-morning trading was getting active. The shining numbers whirred on the board, which sounded like a huge cage of artificial birds. Lard fluctuated between two points, but rye slowly climbed.

He closed his strained, greatly earnest eyes briefly and nodded his Buddha's head, too large to suffer such uncertainties. For several moments of peace he was removed to his small yard in Roxbury.

He breathed in the sugar of the pure morning.

He heard the long phrases of the birds.

No enemy wanted his life.

Wilhelm thought, I will get out of here. I don't belong in New York any more. And he sighed like a sleeper.

Tamkin said, "Excuse me," and left his seat. He could not sit still in the room but passed back and forth between the stocks and com-modities sections. He knew dozens of people and was continually engaging in discussions. Was he giving advice, gathering information, or giving it, or practising – whatever mysterious profession he practised? Hypnotism? Perhaps he could put people in a trance while he talked to them. What a rare, peculiar bird he was, with those pointed shoulders, that bare head, his loose nails, almost claws, and those brown, soft, deadly, heavy eyes.

He spoke of things that mattered, and as very few people did this he could take you by surprise, excite you, move you. Maybe he wished to do good, maybe give himself a lift to a higher level, maybe believe his own prophecies, maybe touch his own heart. Who could tell? He had picked up a lot of strange ideas; Wilhelm could only suspect, he could not say with certainty, that Tamkin hadn't made them his own.

Now Tamkin and he were equal partners, but Tamkin had put up only three hundred dollars. Suppose he did this not only once but five times; then an investment of fifteen hundred dollars gave him five thousand to speculate with. If he had power of attorney in every case, he could shift the money from one account to another. No, the German probably kept an eye on him. Nevertheless it was possible. Calculations like this made Wilhelm feel ill. Obviously Tamkin was a plunger. But how did he get by? He must be in his fifties. How did he support himself? Five years in Egypt; Hollywood before that; Michigan; Ohio; Chicago. A man of fifty has supported himself for at least thirty years. You could be sure that Tamkin had never worked in a factory or in an office. How did he make it? His taste in clothes was horrible, but he didn't buy cheap things. He wore corduroy or velvet shirts from Clyde's, painted neckties, striped socks. There was a slightly acid or pasty smell about his person; for a doctor, he didn't bathe much. Also, Dr Tamkin had a good room at the Gloriana and had had it for about a year. But so was Wilhelm himself a guest, with an unpaid bill at present in his father's box. Did the beautiful girl with the skirts and belts pay him? Was he defrauding his so-called patients? So many questions impossible to answer could not be asked about an honest man. Nor perhaps about a sane man. Was Tamkin a lunatic, then? That sick Mr Perls at breakfast had said that there was no easy way to tell the sane from the mad, and he was right about that in any big city and especially in New York – the end of the world, with its complexity and machinery, bricks and tubes, wires and stones, holes and heights. And was everybody crazy here? What sort of people did you see? Every other man spoke a language entirely his own, which he had figured out by private thinking; he had his own ideas and peculiar ways. If you wanted to talk about a glass of water, you had to start back with God creating the heavens and earth; the apple; Abraham; Moses and Jesus; Rome; the Middle Ages; gunpowder; the Revolution; back to Newton; up to Einstein; then war and 'Lenin and Hitler. After reviewing this and getting it all straight again you could proceed to talk about a glass of water. "I'm fainting, please get me a little water." You were lucky even then to make yourself understood. And this happened over and over and over with everyone you met. You had to translate and translate, explain and explain, back and forth, and it was the punishment of hell itself not to understand or be understood, not to know the crazy from the sane, the wise from the fools, the young from the old or the sick from the well. The fathers were no fathers and the sons no sons. You had to talk with yourself in the daytime and reason with yourself at night. Who else was there to talk to in a city like New York?

A queer look came over Wilhelm's face with its eyes turned up and his silent mouth with its high upper lip. He went several degrees further – when you are like this, dreaming that everybody is outcast, you realize that this must be one of the small matters. There is a larger body, and from this you cannot be separated. The glass of water fades you. You do not go from simple a and simple b to the great x and y, nor does it matter whether you agree about the glass but, far beneath such details, what Tamkin would call the real soul says plain and understandable things to everyone. There sons and fathers are themselves, and a glass of water is only an ornament; it makes a hoop of brightness on the cloth; it is an angel's mouth. There truth for everybody may be found, and confusion is only – only temporary, thought Wilhelm.

The idea of this larger body had been planted in him a few days ago beneath Times Square, when he had gone downtown to pick up tickets for the baseball game on Saturday (a double-header at the Polo Grounds). He was going through an underground corridor, a place he had always hated and hated more than ever now. On the walls between the advertisements were words in chalk: "Sin No More", and "Do Not Eat the Pig", he had particularly noticed. And in the dark tunnel, in the haste, heat, and darkness which disfigure and make freaks and fragments of nose and eyes and teeth, all of a sudden, unsought, a general love for all these imperfect and lurid-looking people burst out in Wilhelm's breast. He loved them. One and all, he passionately loved them. They were his brothers and his sisters. He was imperfect and

68

disfigured himself, but what difference did that make if he was united with them by this blaze of love? And as he walked he began to say, "Oh, my brothers – my brothers and my sisters," blessing them all as well as himself.

So what did it matter how many languages there were, or how hard it was to describe a glass of water? Or matter that a few minutes later he didn't feel anything like a brother toward the man who sold him the tickets?

On that very same afternoon he didn't hold so high an opinion of the same onrush of loving kindness. What did it come to? As they had the capacity and must use it once in a while, people were bound to have such involuntary feelings. It was only another one of those subway things. Like having a hard-on at random. But today, his day of reckoning, he consulted his memory again and thought, I must go back to that. That's the right clue and may do me the most good. Something very big. Truth, like.

The old fellow on the right, Mr Rappaport, was nearly blind and kept asking Wilhelm, "What's the new figure on November wheat? Give me July soy beans too." When you told him he didn't say thank you. He said, "Okay", instead, or, "Check", and turned away until he needed you again. He was very old, older even than Dr Adler, and if you believed Tamkin he had once been the Rockefeller of the chicken business and had retired with a large fortune.

Wilhelm had a queer feeling about the chicken industry, that it was sinister. On the road, he frequently passed chicken farms. Those big, rambling, wooden buildings out in the neglected fields; they were like prisons. The lights burned all night in them to cheat the poor hens into laying. Then the slaughter. Pile all the coops of the slaughtered on end, and in one week they'd go higher than Mount Everest or Mount Serenity. The blood filling the Gulf of Mexico. The chicken shit, acid, burning the earth.

How old – old this Mr Rappaport was! Purple stains were buried in the flesh of his nose, and the cartilage of his ear was twisted like a cabbage heart. Beyond remedy by glasses, his eyes were smoky and faded.

"Read me that soy-bean figure now, boy," he said, and Wilhelm did. He thought perhaps the old man might give him a tip, or some useful advice or information about Tamkin. But no. He only wrote memoranda on a pad, and put the pad in his pocket. He let no one see what he had written. And Wilhelm thought this was the way a man who had grown rich by the murder of millions of animals, little chickens, would act. If there was a life to come he might have to answer for the killing of all those chickens. What if they were waiting? But if there was a life to come, everybody would have to answer. But if there was a life to come, the chickens themselves would be all right.

Well! What stupid ideas he was having this morning. Phooey!

Finally old Rappaport did address a few remarks to Wilhelm. He asked him whether he had reserved his seat in the synagogue for Yom Kippur.

"No," said Wilhelm.

"Well, you better hurry up if you expect to say *Yiskor* for your parents. I never miss."

And Wilhelm thought, Yes, I suppose I should say a prayer for Mother once in a while. His mother had belonged to the Reform congregation. His father had no religion. At the cemetery Wilhelm had paid a man to say a prayer for her. He was among the tombs and he wanted to be tipped for the *El molai rachamin*. "Thou God of Mercy", Wilhelm thought that meant. *B'gan Aden* – "in Paradise". Singing, they drew it out. *B'gan Ay–den*. The broken bench beside the grave made him wish to do something. Wilhelm often prayed in his own manner. He did not go to the synagogue but he would occasionally perform certain devotions, according to his feelings. Now he reflected, In Dad's eyes I am the wrong kind of Jew. He doesn't like the way I act. Only he is the right kind of Jew. Whatever you are, it always turns out to be the wrong kind.

Mr Rappaport grumbled and whiffed at his long cigar, and the board, like a swarm of electrical bees, whirred.

"Since you were in the chicken business, I thought you'd speculate in eggs, Mr Rappaport." Wilhelm, with his warm, panting laugh, sought to charm the old man.

"Oh. Yeah. Loyalty, hey?" said old Rappaport. "I should stick to them. I spent a lot of time amongst chickens. I got to be an expert chicken-sexer. When the chick hatches you have to tell the boys from the girls. It's not easy. You need long, long experience. What do you think, it's a joke? A whole industry depends on it. Yes, now and then I buy a contract of eggs. What have you got today?"

Wilhelm said anxiously, "Lard. Rye."

"Buy? Sell?"

"Bought."

"Uh," said the old man. Wilhelm could not determine what he meant by this. But of course you couldn't expect him to make himself any clearer. It was not in the code to give information to anyone. Sick with desire, Wilhelm waited for Mr Rappaport to make an exception in his case. Just this once! Because it was critical. Silently, by a sort of telepathic concentration, he begged the old man to speak the single word that would save him, give him the merest sign. "Oh, please – please help," he nearly said. If Rappaport would close one eye, or lay his head to one side, or raise his finger and point to a column in the paper or to a figure on his pad. A hint! A hint!

A long perfect ash formed on the end of the cigar, the white ghost of the leaf with all its veins and its fainter pungency. It was ignored, in its beauty, by the old man. For it was beautiful. Wilhelm he ignored as well.

Then Tamkin said to him, "Wilhelm, look at the jump our rye just took."

December rye climbed three points as they tensely watched; the tumblers raced and the machine's lights buzzed.

"A point and a half more, and we can cover the lard losses," said Tamkin. He showed him his calculations on the margin of the *Times*.

"I think you should put in the selling order now. Let's get out with a small loss."

"Get out now? Nothing doing?"

"Why not? Why should we wait?"

"Because," said Tamkin with a smiling, almost openly scoffing look, "you've got to keep your nerve when the market starts to go places. Now's when you can make something."

"I'd get out while the getting's good."

"No, you shouldn't lose your head like this. It's obvious to me what the mechanism is, back in the Chicago market. There's a short supply of December rye. Look, it's just gone up another quarter. We should ride it."

"I'm losing my taste for the gamble," said Wilhelm. "You can't feel safe when it goes up so fast. It's liable to come down just as quick."

Dryly, as though he were dealing with a child, Tamkin told him in a tone of tiring patience, "Now listen, Tommy. I have it diagnosed right. If you wish I should sell I can give the sell order. But this is the difference between healthiness and pathology. One is objective, doesn't change his mind every minute, enjoys the risk element. But that's not the neurotic character. The neurotic character –"

"Damn it, Tamkin!" said Wilhelm roughly. "Cut that out. I don't like it. Leave my character out of consideration. Don't pull any more of that stuff on me. I tell you I don't like it."

Tamkin therefore went no further; he backed down. "I meant," he said, softer, "that as a salesman you are basically an artist type. The seller is in the visionary sphere of the business function. And then you're an actor, too."

"No matter what type I am –" An angry and yet weak sweetness rose into Wilhelm's throat. He coughed as though he had the flu. It was twenty years since he had appeared on the screen as an extra. He blew the bagpipes in a film called *Annie Laurie*. Annie had come to warn the young Laird; he would not believe her and called the bagpipers to drown her out. He made fun of her while she wrung her hands. Wilhelm, in a kilt, barelegged, blew and blew and blew and not a sound came out. Of course all the music was recorded. He fell sick with the flu after that and still suffered sometimes from chest weakness.

"Something stuck in your throat?" said Tamkin. "I think maybe you are too disturbed to think clearly. You should try some of my 'here-and-now' mental exercises. It stops you from thinking so much about the future and the past and cuts down confusion."

"Yes, yes, yes, yes," said Wilhelm, his eyes fixed on December rye.

"Nature only knows one thing, and that's the present. Present, present, eternal present, like a big, huge, giant wave – colossal, bright and beautiful, full of life and death, climbing into the sky, standing in the seas. You must go along with the actual, the Here-and-Now, the glory –"

. . . chest weakness, Wilhelm's recollection went on. Margaret nursed him. They had two rooms of furniture, which was later seized. She sat on the bed and read to him. He made her read for days, and she read stories, poetry, everything in the house. He felt dizzy, stifled when he tried to smoke. They had him wear a flannel vest.

Come then, Sorrow!
Sweetest Sorrow!
Like an own babe I nurse thee on my breast!

Why did he remember that? Why?

"You have to pick out something that's in the actual, immediate present moment," said Tamkin. "And say to yourself here-and-now, here-and-now, here-and-now, "Where am I?" "Here." "When is it?" "Now." Take an object or a person. Anybody, "Here and now I see a person." "Here and now I see a man." "Here and now I see a man sitting on a chair." Take me, for instance. Don't let your mind wander. "Here and now I see a man in a brown suit. Here and now I see a corduroy shirt." You have to narrow it down, one item at a time, and not let your imagination shoot ahead. Be in the present. Grasp the hour, the moment, the instant."

Is he trying to hypnotize or con me? Wilhelm wondered. To take my mind off selling? But even if I'm back at seven hundred bucks, then where am I?

As if in prayer, his lids coming down with raised veins, frayed out, on his significant eyes, Tamkin said, ' "Here and now I see a button. Here and now I see the thread that sews the button. Here and now I see the green thread." ' Inch by inch he contemplated himself in order to show Wilhelm how calm it would make him. But Wilhelm was hearing Margaret's voice as she read, somewhat unwillingly.

Come then, Sorrow!
. . . .
I thought to leave thee,
And deceive thee,
But now of all the world I love thee best.

Then Mr Rappaport's old hand pressed his thigh, and he said, "What's my wheat? Those damn guys are blocking the way. I can't see."

6

Rye was still ahead when they went out to lunch, and lard was holding its own.

They are in the cafeteria with the gilded front. There was the same art inside as outside. The food looked sumptuous. Whole fishes were framed like pictures with carrots, and the salads were like terraced landscapes or like Mexican pyramids; slices of lemon and onion and radishes were like sun and moon and stars; the cream pies were about a foot thick and the cakes swollen as if sleepers had baked them in their dreams.

"What'll you have?" said Tamkin.

"Not much. I ate a big breakfast. I'll find a table. Bring me some yogurt and crackers and a cup of tea. I don't want to spend much time over lunch."

Tamkin said, "You've got to eat."

Finding an empty place at this hour was not easy. The old people idled and gossiped over their coffee. The elderly ladies were rouged and mascaraed and hennaed and used blue hair rinse and eye shadow and wore costume jewellery, and many of them were proud and stared at you with expressions that did not belong to their age. Were there no longer any respectable old ladies who knitted and cooked and looked after their grandchildren? Wilhelm's grandmother had dressed him in a sailor suit and danced him on her knee, blew on the porridge for him and said, "Admiral, you must eat." But what was the use of remembering this so late in the day?

He managed to find a table, and Dr Tamkin came along with a tray piled with plates and cups. He had Yankee pot roast, purple cabbage, potatoes, a big slice of watermelon, and two cups of coffee. Wilhelm could not even swallow his yogurt. His chest pained him still.

At once Tamkin involved him in a lengthy discussion. Did he do it to stall Wilhelm and prevent him from selling out the rye – or to recover the ground lost when he had made Wilhelm angry by hints about the neurotic character? Or did he have no purpose except to talk?

"I think you worry a lot too much about what your wife and your father will say. Do they matter so much?"

Wilhelm replied, "A person can become tired of looking himself over and trying to fix himself up. You can spend the entire second half of your life recovering from the mistakes of the first half."

"I believe your dad told me he had some money to leave you."

"He probably does have something."

"A lot?"

"Who can tell," said Wilhelm guardedly.

"You ought to think over what you'll do with it."

"I may be too feeble to do anything by the time I get it. If I get anything."

"A thing like this you ought to plan out carefully. Invest it properly." He began to unfold schemes whereby you bought bonds, and used the bonds as security to buy something else and thereby earned twelve per cent safely on your money. Wilhelm failed to follow the details. Tamkin said, "If he made you a gift now, you wouldn't have to pay the inheritance taxes."

Bitterly, Wilhelm told him, "My father's death blots out all other considerations from his mind. He forces me to think about it, too. Then he hates me because he succeeds. When I get desperate – of course I think about money. But I don't want anything to happen to him. I certainly don't want him to die." Tamkin's brown eyes glittered shrewdly at him. "You don't believe it. Maybe it's not psychological. But on my word of honour. A joke is a joke, but I won't want to joke about stuff like this. When he dies, I'll be robbed, like I'll have no more father."

"You love your old man?"

Wilhelm grasped at this. "Of course, of course I love him. My father. My mother –" As he said this there was a great pull at the very centre of his soul. When a fish strikes the line you feel the live force in your hand. A mysterious being beneath the water, driven by hunger, has taken the hook and rushes away and fights, writhing. Wilhelm never identified what struck within him. It did not reveal itself. It got away.

And Tamkin, the confuser of the imagination, began to tell, or to fabricate, the strange history of *his* father. "He was a great singer," he said. "He left us five kids because he fell in love with an opera soprano. I never held it against him, but admired the way he followed the life-principle. I wanted to do the same. Because of unhappiness, at a certain age, the brain starts to die back." (True, true! thought Wilhelm.) "Twenty years later I was doing experiments in Eastman Kodak, Rochester, and I found the old fellow. He had five more children." (False, false!) "He wept; he was ashamed. I had nothing against him. I naturally felt strange."

"My dad is something of a stranger to me, too," said Wilhelm, and he began to muse. Where is the familiar person he used to be? Or I used to be? Catherine – she won't even talk to me any more, my own sister. It may not be so much my trouble that Papa turns his back on as my confusion. It's too much. The ruins of life, and on top of that confusion – chaos and old night. Is it an easier farewell for Dad if we don't part friends? He should maybe do it angrily – "Blast you with my curse!" And why, Wilhelm further asked, should he or anybody else pity me; or why should I be pitied sooner than another fellow? It is my childish mind that thinks people are ready to give it just because you need it.

Then Wilhelm began to think about his own two sons and to wonder how he appeared to them, and what they would think of him. Right now he had an advantage through baseball. When he went to fetch them, to go to Ebbets Field, though, he was not himself. He put on a front but he felt as if he had swallowed a fistful of sand. The strange, familiar house, horribly awkward; the dog, Scissors, rolled over on his back and barked and whined. Wilhelm acted as if there were nothing irregular, but a weary heaviness came over him. On the way to Flatbush he would think up anecdotes about old Pigtown and Charlie Ebbets for the boys and reminiscences of the old stars, but it was very heavy going. They did not know how much he cared for them. No. It hurt him greatly and he blamed Margaret for turning them against him. She wanted to ruin him, while she wore the mask of kindness. Up in Roxbury he had to go and explain to the priest, who was not sympathetic. They don't care about individuals, their rules come first. Olive said she would marry him outside the Church when he was divorced. But Margaret would not let go. Olive's father was a pretty decent old guy, an osteopath, and he understood what it was all about. Finally he said, "See here, I have to advise Olive. She is asking me. I am mostly a freethinker myself, but the girl has to live in this town." And by now Wilhelm and Olive had had a great many troubles and she was beginning to dread his days in Roxbury, she said. He trembled at offending this small, pretty, dark girl whom he adored. When she would get up late on Sunday morning she would wake him almost in tears at being late for Mass. He would try to help her hitch her garters and smooth out her slip and dress and even put on her hat with shaky hands; then he would rush her to church and drive in second gear in his forgetful way, trying to apologize and to calm her. She got out a block from church to avoid gossip. Even so she loved him, and she would have married him if he had obtained the divorce. But Margaret must have sensed this. Margaret would tell him he did not really want a divorce; he was afraid of it. He cried, "Take everything I've got, Margaret. Let me go to Reno. Don't you want to marry again?" No. She went out with other men, but took his money. She lived in order to punish him.

Dr Tamkin told Wilhelm, "Your dad is jealous of you." 5

Wilhelm smiled. "Of *me*? That's rich."

"Sure. People are always jealous of a man who leaves his wife."

"Oh," said Wilhelm scornfully. "When it comes to wives he wouldn't have to envy me."

"Yes, and your wife envies you, too. She thinks, He's free and goes 10 with young women. Is she getting old?"

"Not exactly old," said Wilhelm, whom the mention of his wife made sad. Twenty years ago, in a neat blue wool suit, in a soft hat made of the same cloth – he could plainly see her. He stooped his yellow head and looked under the hat at her clear, simple face, her living eyes moving, 15 her straight small nose, her jaw beautifully, painfully clear in its form. It was a cool day, but he smelled the odour of pines in the sun, in the granite canyon. Just south of Santa Barbara, this was.

"She's forty-some years old," he said.

"I was married to a lush," said Tamkin. "A painful alcoholic. I 20 couldn't take her out to dinner because she'd say she was going to the ladies' toilet and disappear into the bar. I'd ask the bartenders they shouldn't serve her. But I love her deeply. She was the most spiritual woman of my entire experience."

"Where is she now?" 25

"Drowned," said Tamkin. "At Provincetown, Cape Cod. It must have been suicide. She was that way – suicidal. I tried everything in my power to cure her. Because," said Tamkin, "my real calling is to be a healer. I get wounded. I suffer from it. I would like to escape from the sicknesses of others, but I can't. I am only on loan to myself, so to speak. 30 I belong to humanity."

Liar! Wilhelm inwardly called him. Nasty lies. He invented a woman and killed her off and then called himself a healer, and made himself so earnest he looked like a bad-natured sheep. He's a puffed-up little bogus and humbug with smelly feet. A doctor! A doctor would wash himself. 35 He believes he's making a terrific impression, and he practically invites you to take off your hat when he talks about himself; and he thinks he has an imagination, but he hasn't, neither is he smart.

Then what am I doing with him here, and why did I give him the seven hundred dollars? thought Wilhelm.

Oh, this was a day of reckoning. It was a day, he thought, on which, willing or not, he would take a good close look at the truth. He breathed hard and his misshapen hat came low upon his congested dark blond face. A rude look. Tamkin was a charlatan, and furthermore he was desperate. And furthermore, Wilhelm had always known this about him. But he appeared to have worked it out at the back of his mind that Tamkin for thirty or forty years had gotten through many a tight place, that he would get through this crisis too and bring him, Wilhelm, to safety also. And Wilhelm realized that he was on Tamkin's back. It made him feel that he had virtually left the ground and was riding upon the other man. He was in the air. It was for Tamkin to take the steps.

The doctor, if he was a doctor, did not look anxious. But then his face did not have much variety. Talking always about spontaneous emotion and open receptors and free impulses he was about as expressive as a pincushion. When his hypnotic spell failed, his big underlip made him look weak-minded. Fear stared from his eyes, sometimes, so humble as to make you sorry for him. Once or twice Wilhelm had seen that look. Like a dog, he thought. Perhaps he didn't look it now, but he was very nervous. Wilhelm knew, but he could not afford to recognize this too openly. The doctor needed a little room, a little time. He should not be pressed now. So Tamkin went on, telling his tales.

Wilhelm said to himself, I am on his back – his back. I gambled seven hundred bucks, so I must take this ride. I have to go along with him. It's too late. I can't get off.

"You know," Tamkin said, "that blind old man Rappaport – he's pretty close to totally blind – is one of the most interesting personalities around here. If you could only get him to tell his true story. It's fascinating. This is what he told me. You often hear about bigamists with a secret life. But this old man never hid anything from anybody. He's a regular patriarch. Now, I'll tell you what he did. He had two whole families, separate and apart, one in Williamsburg and the other in the Bronx. The two wives knew about each other. The wife in the Bronx was younger; she's close to seventy now. When he got sore at one wife he went to live with the other one. Meanwhile he ran his chicken business in New Jersey. By one wife he had four kids, and by the other six. They're all grown, but they never have met their half-brothers and sisters and don't want to. The whole bunch of them are listed in the telephone book."

"I can't believe it," said Wilhelm.

"He told me this himself. And do you know what else? While he had his eyesight he used to read a lot, but the only books he would read were by Theodore Roosevelt. He had a set in each of the places where he lived, and he brought his kids up on those books."

"Please," said Wilhelm, "don't feed me any more of this stuff, will you? Kindly do not —"

"In telling you this," said Tamkin with one of his hypnotic subtleties, "I do have a motive. I want you to see how some people free themselves from morbid guilt feelings and follow their instincts. Innately, the female knows how to cripple by sickening a man with guilt. It is a very special *de*struct, and she sends her curse to make a fellow impotent. As if she says, 'Unless I allow it, you will never more be a man.' But men like my old dad or Mr Rappaport answer, 'Woman, what art thou to me?' You can't do that yet. You're a half-way case. You want to follow your instinct, but you're too worried still. For instance, about your kids —"

"Now look here," said Wilhelm, stamping his feet. "One thing! Don't bring up my boys. Just lay off."

"I was only going to say that they are better off than with conflicts in the home."

"I'm deprived of my children." Wilhelm bit his lip. It was too late to turn away. The anguish struck him. "I pay and pay. I never see them. They grow up without me. She makes them like herself. She'll bring them up to be my enemies. Please let's not talk about this."

But Tamkin said, "Why do you let her make you suffer so? It defeats the original object in leaving her. Don't play her game. Now, Wilhelm, I'm trying to do you some good. I want to tell you, don't marry suffering. Some people do. They get married to it, and sleep and eat together, just as husband and wife. If they go with joy they think it's adultery."

When Wilhelm heard this he had, in spite of himself, to admit that there was a great deal in Tamkin's words. Yes, thought Wilhelm, suffering is the only kind of life they are sure they can have, and if they quit suffering they're afraid they'll have nothing. He knows it. This time the faker knows what he's talking about.

Looking at Tamkin he believed he saw all this confessed from his usually barren face. Yes, yes, he too. One hundred falsehoods, but at last one truth. Howling like a wolf from the city window. No one can bear it any more. Everyone is so full of it that at last everybody must proclaim it. It! It!

Then suddenly Wilhelm rose and said, "That's enough of this. Tamkin, let's go back to the market."

"I haven't finished my melon."

"Never mind that. You've had enough to eat. I want to go back."

Dr Tamkin slid the two checks across the table. "Who paid yesterday? It's your turn, I think."

It was not until they were leaving the cafeteria that Wilhelm remembered definitely that he had paid yesterday too. But it wasn't worth arguing about.

Tamkin kept repeating as they walked down the street that there were many who were dedicated to suffering. But he told Wilhelm, "I'm optimistic in your case, and I have seen a world of maladjustment. There's hope for you. You don't really want to destroy yourself. You're trying hard to keep your feelings open, Wilhelm. I can see it. Seven per cent of this country is committing suicide by alcohol. Another three, maybe narcotics. Another sixty just fading away into dust by boredom. Twenty more who have sold their souls to the Devil. Then there's a small percentage of those who want to live. That's the only significant thing in the whole world of today. Those are the only two classes of people there are. Some want to live, but the great majority don't." This fantastic Tamkin began to surpass himself. "They don't. Or else, why these wars? I'll tell you more," he said. "The love of the dying amounts to one thing; they want you to die with them. It's because they love you. Make no mistake."

True, true! thought Wilhelm, profoundly moved by these revelations. How does he know these things? How can he be such a jerk, and even perhaps an operator, a swindler, and understand so well what gives? I believe what he says. It simplifies much – everything. People are dropping like flies. I am trying to stay alive and work too hard at it. That's what's turning my brains. This working hard defeats its own end. At what point should I start over? Let me go back a ways and try once more.

Only a few hundred yards separated the cafeteria from the broker's, and within that short space Wilhelm turned again, in measurable degrees, from these wide considerations to the problems of the moment. The closer he approached to the market, the more Wilhelm had to think about money.

They passed the newsreel theatre where the ragged shoeshine kids called after them. The same old bearded man with his bandaged beggar face and his tiny ragged feet and the old press clipping on his fiddle case to prove he had once been a concert violinist, pointed his bow at Wilhelm, saying, "You!" Wilhelm went by with worried eyes, bent on crossing Seventy-second Street. In full tumult the great afternoon current raced for Columbus Circle, where the mouth of mid-town stood open and the skyscrapers gave back the yellow fire of the sun.

As they approached the polished stone of the new office building, Dr Tamkin said, "Well, isn't that old Rappaport by the door? I think he should carry a white cane, but he will never admit there's a single thing the matter with his eyes."

Mr Rappaport did not stand well; his knees were sunk, while his pelvis only half filled his trousers. His suspenders held them, gaping.

He stopped Wilhelm with an extended hand, having somehow recognized him. In his deep voice he commanded him, "Take me to the cigar store."

"You want me –? Tamkin!" Wilhelm whispered, "You take him."

Tamkin shook his head. "He wants you. Don't refuse the old gentleman." Significantly he said in a lower voice, "This minute is another instance of the "here-and-now". You have to live in this very minute, and you don't want to. A man asks you for help. Don't think of the market. It won't run away. Show your respect to the old boy. Go ahead. That may be more valuable."

"Take me," said the old chicken merchant again.

Greatly annoyed, Wilhelm wrinkled his face at Tamkin. He took the old man's big but light elbow at the bone. "Well, let's step on it," he said. "Or wait – I want to have a look at the board first to see how we're doing."

But Tamkin had already started Mr Rappaport forward. He was walking, and he scolded Wilhelm, saying, "Don't leave me standing in the middle of the sidewalk. I'm afraid to get knocked over."

"Let's get a move on. Come." Wilhelm urged him as Tamkin went into the broker's.

The traffic seemed to come down Broadway out of the sky, where the hot spokes of the sun rolled from the south. Hot, stony odours rose from the subway grating in the street.

"These teen-age hoodlums worry me. I'm ascared of these Puerto Rican kids, and these young characters who take dope," said Mr Rappaport. "They go around all hopped up."

"Hoodlums?" said Wilhelm. "I went to the cemetery and my mother's stone bench was split. I could have broken somebody's neck for that. Which store do you go to?"

"Across Broadway. That La Magnita sign next door to the Automat."

"What's the matter with this store here on this side?"

"They don't carry my brand, that's what's the matter."

Wilhelm cursed, but checked the words.

"What are you talking?"

"Those damn taxis," said Wilhelm. "They want to run everybody down."

They entered the cool, odorous shop. Mr Rappaport put away his large cigars with great care in various pockets while Wilhelm muttered, "Come on, you old creeper. What a poky old character! The whole world waits on him." Rappaport did not offer Wilhelm a cigar, but, holding one up, he asked, "What do you say at the size of these, huh? They're Churchill-type cigars."

He barely crawls along, thought Wilhelm. His pants are dropping off because he hasn't got enough flesh for them to stick to. He's almost blind, and covered with spots, but this old man still makes money in the market. Is loaded with dough, probably. And I bet he doesn't give his children any. Some of them must be in their fifties. This is what keeps middle-aged men as children. He's master over the dough. Think – just think! Who controls everything? Old men of this type. Without needs. They don't need therefore they have. I need, therefore I don't have. That would be too easy.

"I'm older even than Churchill," said Rappaport.

Now he wanted to talk! But if you asked him a question in the market, he couldn't be bothered to answer.

"I bet you are," said Wilhelm. "Come, let's get going."

"I was a fighter, too, like Churchill," said the old man. "When we licked Spain I went into the Navy. Yes, I was a gob that time. What did I have to lose? Nothing. After the battle of San Juan Hill, Teddy Roosevelt kicked me off the beach."

"Come, watch the kerb," said Wilhelm.

"I was curious and wanted to see what went on. I didn't have no business there, but I took a boat and rowed myself to the beach. Two of our guys was dead, layin' under the American flag to keep the flies off. So I says to the guy on duty, there, who was the sentry, 'Let's have a look at these guys. I want to see what went on here,' and he says, 'Naw,' but I talked him into it. So he took off the flag and there were these two tall guys, both gentlemen, lying in their boots. They was very tall. The two of them had long moustaches. They were high-society boys. I think one of them was called Fish, from up the Hudson, a big-shot family. When I looked up, there was Teddy Roosevelt, with his hat off, and he was looking at these fellows, the only ones who got killed there. Then he says to me, 'What's the Navy want here? Have you got orders?' 'No, sir,' I says to him. 'Well, get the hell off the beach, then.' "

Old Rappaport was very proud of this memory. "Everything he said had such snap, such class. Man! I love that Teddy Roosevelt," he said, "I love him!"

Ah, what people are! He is almost not with us, and his life is nearly gone, but T. R. once yelled at him, so he loves him. I guess it is love, too. Wilhelm smiled. So maybe the rest of Tamkin's story was true, about the ten children and the wives and the telephone directory.

He said, "Come on, come on, Mr Rappaport," and hurried the old man back by the large hollow elbow; he gripped it through the thin cotton cloth. Re-entering the brokerage office where under the lights the tumblers were speeding with the clack of drumsticks upon wooden blocks, more than ever resembling a Chinese theatre, Wilhelm strained his eyes to see the board.

The lard figures were unfamiliar. That amount couldn't be lard! They must have put the figures in the wrong slot. He traced the line back to the margin. It was down to .19, and had dropped twenty points since noon. And what about the contract of rye? It had sunk back to its earlier position, and they had lost their chance to sell.

Old Mr Rappaport said to Wilhelm, "Read me my wheat figure."

"Oh, leave me alone for a minute," he said, and positively hid his face from the old man behind one hand. He looked for Tamkin, Tamkin's bald head, or Tamkin with his grey straw and the cocoa-coloured band. He couldn't see him. Where was he? The seats next to Rowland were taken by strangers. He thrust himself over the one on the aisle, Mr Rappaport's former place, and pushed at the back of the chair until the new occupant, a red-headed man with a thin, determined face, leaned forward to get out of his way but would not surrender the seat. "Where's Tamkin?" Wilhelm asked Rowland.

"Gee, I don't know. Is anything wrong?"

"You must have seen him. He came in a while back."

"No, but I didn't."

Wilhelm fumbled out a pencil from the top pocket of his coat and began to make calculations. His very fingers were numb, and in his agitation he was afraid he made mistakes with the decimal points and went over the substractions and multiplication like a schoolboy at an exam. His heart, accustomed to many sorts of crisis, was now in a new panic. And, as he had dreaded, he was wiped out. It was unnecessary to ask the German manager. He could see for himself that the electronic book-keeping device must have closed him out. The manager probably had known that Tamkin wasn't to be trusted, and on that first day he might have warned him. But you couldn't expect him to interfere.

"You get hit?" said Mr Rowland.

And Wilhelm, quite coolly, said, "Oh, it could have been worse, I guess." He put the piece of paper into his pocket with its cigarette butts and packets of pills. The lie helped him out – although, for a moment, he was afraid he would cry. But he hardened himself. The hardening effort made a violent, vertical pain go through his chest, like that caused by a pocket of air under the collar bones. To the old chicken millionaire, who by this time had become acquainted with the drop in rye and lard, he also denied that anything serious had happened. "It's just one of those temporary slumps. Nothing to be scared about," he said, and remained in possession of himself. His need to cry, like someone in a crowd, pushed and jostled and abused him from behind, and Wilhelm did not dare turn. He said to himself, I will not cry in front of these people. I'll be damned if I'll break down in front of them like a kid, even though I never expect to see them again. No! No! And yet his unshed tears rose and rose and he looked like a man about to drown. But when they talked to him, he answered very distinctly. He tried to speak proudly.

". . . going away?" he heard Rowland ask.

"What?"

"I thought you might be going away too. Tamkin said he was going to Maine this summer for his vacation."

"Oh, going away?"

Wilhelm broke off and went to look for Tamkin in the men's toilet. Across the corridor was the room where the machinery of the board was housed. It hummed and whirred like mechanical birds, and the tubes glittered in the dark. A couple of businessmen with cigarettes in their fingers were having a conversation in the lavatory. At the top of the closet door sat a grey straw hat with a cocoa-coloured band. "Tamkin," said Wilhelm. He tried to identify the feet below the door. "Are you in there, Doctor Tamkin?" he said with stifled anger. "Answer me. It's Wilhelm."

The hat was taken down, the latch lifted, and a stranger came out who looked at him with annoyance.

"You waiting?" said one of the businessmen. He was warning Wilhelm that he was out of turn.

"Me? Not me," said Wilhelm. "I'm looking for a fellow."

Bitterly angry, he said to himself that Tamkin would pay him the two hundred dollars at least, his share of the original deposit. "And before he takes the train to Maine, too. Before he spends a penny on vacation – that liar! We went into this as equal partners."

7

I was the man beneath; Tamkin was on my back, and I thought I was on his. He made me carry him, too, besides Margaret. Like this they ride on me with hoofs and claws. Tear me to pieces, stamp on me and break my bones.

Once more the hoary old fiddler pointed his bow at Wilhelm as he hurried by. Wilhelm rejected his begging and denied the omen. He dodged heavily through traffic and with his quick, small steps ran up the lower stairway of the Gloriana Hotel with its dark-tinted mirrors, kind to people's defects. From the lobby he phoned Tamkin's room, and when no one answered he took the elevator up. A rouged woman in her fifties with a mink stole led three tiny dogs on a leash, high-strung creatures with prominent black eyes, like dwarf deer, and legs like twigs. This was the eccentric Estonian lady who had been moved with her pets to the twelfth floor.

She identified Wilhelm. "You are Doctor Adler's son," she said.

Formally, he nodded.

"I am a dear friend of your father."

He stood in the corner and would not meet her glance, and she thought he was snubbing her and made a mental note to speak of it to the doctor.

The linen-wagon stood at Tamkin's door, and the chambermaid's key with its big brass tongue was in the lock.

"Has Doctor Tamkin been here?" he asked her.

"No, I haven't seen him."

Wilhelm came in, however, to look around. He examined the photos on the desk, trying to connect the faces with the strange people in Tamkin's stories. Big, heavy volumes were stacked under the double-pronged TV aerial. *Science and Sanity,* he read, and there were several books of poetry. The *Wall Street Journal* hung in separate sheets from the bed-table under the weight of the silver water jug. A bathrobe with lightning streaks of red and white was laid across the foot of the bed with a pair of expensive batik pyjamas. It was a box of a room, but from the windows you saw the river as far uptown as the bridge, as far downtown as Hoboken. What lay between was deep, azure, dirty, complex, crystal, rusty, with the red bones of new apartments rising on the bluffs of New Jersey, and huge liners in their berths, the tugs with matted beards of cordage. Even the brackish tidal river smell rose this high, like the smell of mop water. From every side he heard pianos, and the voices of men and women singing scales and opera, all mixed, and the sounds of pigeons on the ledges.

Again Wilhelm took the phone. "Can you locate Doctor Tamkin in the lobby for me?" he asked. And when the operator reported that she could not, Wilhelm gave the number of his father's room, but Dr Adler was not in either. "Well, please give me the masseur. I say the massage room. Don't you understand me? The men's health club. Yes, Max Schilper's – how am I supposed to know the name of it?"

There a strange voice said, "Toktor Adler?" It was the old Czech prizefighter with the deformed nose and ears who was attendant down there and gave out soap, sheets and sandals. He went away. A hollow endless silence followed. Wilhelm flickered the receiver with his nails, whistled into it, but could not summon either the attendant or the operator.

The maid saw him examining the bottles of pills on Tamkin's table and seemed suspicious of him. He was running low on Phenaphen pills and was looking for something else. But he swallowed one of his own tablets and went out and rang again for the elevator. He went down to the health club. Through the steamy windows, when he emerged, he saw the reflection of the swimming-pool swirling green at the bottom of the lowest stairway. He went through the locker-room curtains. Two men wrapped in towels were playing Ping-pong. They were awkward and the ball bounded high. The Negro in the toilet was shining shoes. He did not know Dr Adler by name, and Wilhelm descended to the massage room. On the tables naked men were lying. It was not a brightly lighted place, and it was very hot, and under the white faint moons of the ceiling shone pale skins. Calendar pictures of pretty girls dressed in tiny fringes were pinned on the wall. On the first table, eyes deeply shut in heavy silent luxury lay a man with a full square beard and short legs, stocky and black-haired. He might have been an orthodox Russian. Wrapped in a sheet, waiting, the man beside him was newly shaved and red from the steambath. He had a big happy face and was dreaming. And after him was an athlete, strikingly muscled, powerful and young, with a strong white curve to his genital and a half-angry smile on his mouth. Dr Adler was on the fourth table, and Wilhelm stood over his father's pale, slight body. His ribs were narrow and small, his belly round, white, and high. It had its own being, like something separate. His thighs were weak, the muscles of his arms had fallen, his throat was creased.

The masseur in his undershirt bent and whispered in his ear, "It's your son," and Dr Adler opened his eyes into Wilhelm's face. At once he saw the trouble in it, and by an instantaneous reflex he removed himself from the danger of contagion, and he said serenely, "Well, have you taken my advice, Wilky?"

"Oh, Dad," said Wilhelm.

"To take a swim and get a massage?"

"Did you get my note?" said Wilhelm.

"Yes, but I'm afraid you'll have to ask somebody else, because I can't.

I had no idea you were so low on funds. How did you let it happen? Didn't you lay anything aside?"

"Oh, please, Dad," said Wilhelm, almost bringing his hands together in a clasp.

5 "I'm sorry," said the doctor, "I really am. But I have set up a rule. I've thought about it, I believe it is a good rule, and I don't want to change it. You haven't acted wisely. What's the matter?"

"Everything. Just everything. What isn't? I did have a little, but I haven't been very smart."

10 "You took some gamble? You lost it? Was it Tamkin? I told you, Wilky, not to build on that Tamkin. Did you? I suspect —"

"Yes, Dad, I'm afraid I trusted him."

Dr Adler surrendered his arm to the masseur, who was using wintergreen oil.

15 "Trusted! And got taken?"

"I'm afraid I kind of —" Wilhelm glanced at the masseur but he was absorbed in his work. He probably did not listen to conversations. "I did. I might as well say it. I should have listened to you."

"Well, I won't remind you how often I warned you. It must be very 20 painful."

"Yes, Father, it is."

"I don't know how many times you have to be burned in order to learn something. The same mistakes, over and over."

"I couldn't agree with you more," said Wilhelm with a face of 25 despair. "You're so right, Father. It's the same mistakes, and I get burned again and again. I can't seem to — I'm stupid, Dad, I just can't breathe. My chest is all up — I feel choked. I just simply can't catch my breath."

He stared at his father's nakedness. Presently he became aware that 30 Dr Adler was making an effort to keep his temper. He was on the verge of an explosion. Wilhelm hung his face and said, "Nobody likes bad luck, eh, Dad?"

"So! It's bad luck, now. A minute ago it was stupidity."

"It is stupidity — it's some of both. It's true that I can't learn. But I —"

35 "I don't want to listen to the details," said his father. "And I want you to understand that I'm too old to take on new burdens. I'm just too old to do it. And people who will just wait for help — must *wait* for help. They have got to stop waiting."

"It isn't all a question of money – there are other things a father can give to a son." He lifted up his grey eyes and his nostrils grew wide with a look of suffering appeal that stirred his father even more deeply against him.

He warningly said to him, "Look out, Wilky, you're tiring my patience very much."

"I try not to. But one word from you, just a word, would go a long way. I've never asked you for very much. But you are not a kind man, Father. You don't give the little bit I beg you for."

He recognized that his father was now furiously angry. Dr Adler started to say something, and then raised himself and gathered the sheet over him as he did so. His mouth opened, wide, dark, twisted, and he said to Wilhelm, "You want to make yourself into my cross. But I am not going to pick up a cross. I'll see you dead, Wilky, by Christ, before I let you do that to me."

"Father, listen! Listen!"

"Go away from me now. It's torture for me to look at you, you slob!" cried Dr Adler.

Wilhelm's blood rose up madly, in anger equal to his father's, but then it sank down and left him helplessly captive to misery. He said stiffly, and with a strange sort of formality, "Okay, Dad. That'll be enough. That's about all we should say." And he stalked out heavily by the door adjacent to the swimming-pool and the steam room, and laboured up two long flights from the basement. Once more he took the elevator to the lobby on the mezzanine.

He inquired at the desk for Dr Tamkin.

The clerk said, "No, I haven't seen him. But I think there's something in the box for you."

"Me? Give it here," said Wilhelm and opened a telephone message from his wife. It read, "Please phone Mrs Wilhelm on return. Urgent."

Whenever he received an urgent message from his wife he was always thrown into a great fear for the children. He ran to the phone booth, spilled out the change from his pockets on to the little curved steel shelf under the telephone, and dialled the Digby number.

"Yes?" said his wife. Scissors barked in the parlour.

"Margaret?"

"Yes, hello." They never exchanged any other greeting. She instantly knew his voice.

"The boys all right?"

"They're out on their bicycles. Why shouldn't they be all right? Scissors, quiet!"

"Your message scared me," he said. "I wish you wouldn't make "urgent" so common."

"I had something to tell you."

Her familiar unbending voice awakened in him a kind of hungry longing, not for Margaret but for the peace he had once known.

"You sent me a post-dated cheque," she said. "I can't allow that. It's already five days past the first. You dated your cheque for the twelfth."

"Well, I have no money. I haven't got it. You can't send me to prison for that. I'll be lucky if I can raise it by the twelfth."

She answered, "You better get it, Tommy."

"Yes? What for?" he said. "Tell me. For the sake of what? To tell lies about me to everyone? You –"

She cut him off. "You know what for. I've got the boys to bring up."

Wilhelm in the narrow booth broke into a heavy sweat. He dropped his head and shrugged while with his fingers he arranged nickels, dimes, and quarters in rows. "I'm doing my best," he said. "I've had some bad luck. As a matter of fact, it's been so bad that I don't know where I am. I couldn't tell you what day of the week this is. I can't think straight. I'd better not even try. This has been one of those days, Margaret. May I never live to go through another like it. I mean that with all my heart. So I'm not going to try to do any thinking today. Tomorrow I'm going to see some guys. One is a sales manager. The other is in television. But not to act," he hastily added. "On the business end."

"That's just some more of your talk, Tommy," she said. "You ought to patch things up with Rojax Corporation. They'd take you back. You've got to stop thinking like a youngster."

"What do you mean?"

"Well," she said, measured and unbending, remorselessly unbending, "you still think like a youngster. But you can't do that any more. Every other day you want to make a new start. But in eighteen years you'll be eligible for retirement. Nobody wants to hire a new man of your age."

"I know. But listen, you don't have to sound so hard. I can't get on my knees to them. And really you don't have to sound so hard. I haven't done you so much harm."

"Tommy, I have to chase you and ask you for money that you owe us, and I hate it."

She hated also to be told that her voice was hard.

"I'm making an effort to control myself," she told him.

He could picture her, her greying bangs cut with strict fixity above her pretty, decisive face. She prided herself on being fair-minded. We could not bear, he thought, to know what we do. Even though blood is spilled. Even though the breath of life is taken from someone's nostrils. This is the way of the weak; quiet and fair. And then smash! They smash!

"Rojax take me back? I'd have to crawl back. They don't need me. After so many years I should have got stock in the firm. How can I support the three of you, and live myself, on half the territory? And why should I even try when you won't lift a finger to help? I sent you back to school, didn't I? At that time you said —"

His voice was rising. She did not like that and intercepted him. "You misunderstood me," she said.

"You must realize you're killing me. You can't be as blind as all that. Thou shalt not kill! Don't you remember that?"

She said, "You're just raving now. When you calm down it'll be different. I have great confidence in your earning ability."

"Margaret, you don't grasp the situation. You'll have to get a job."

"Absolutely not. I'm not going to have two young children running loose."

"They're not babies," Wilhelm said. "Tommy is fourteen. Paulie is going to be ten."

"Look," Margaret said in her deliberate manner. "We can't continue this conservation if you're going to yell so, Tommy. They're at a dangerous age. There are teen-aged gangs — the parents working, or the families broken up."

Once again she was reminding him that it was he who had left her. She had the bringing up of the children as her burden, while he must expect to pay the price of his freedom.

Freedom! he thought with consuming bitterness. Ashes in his mouth, not freedom. Give me my children. For they are mine too.

Can you be the woman I lived with? he started to say. Have you forgotten that we slept so long together? Must you now deal with me like this, and have no mercy?

He would be better off with Margaret again than he was today. This was what she wanted to make him feel, and she drove it home. "Are you in misery?" she was saying. "But you have deserved it." And he could not return to her any more than he could beg Rojax to take him back. If it cost him his life, he could not. Margaret had ruined him with Olive. She hit him and hit him, beat him, battered him, wanted to beat the very life out of him.

"Margaret, I want you please to reconsider about work. You have that degree now. Why did I pay your tuition?"

"Because it seemed practical. But it isn't. Growing boys need parental authority and a home."

He begged her, "Margaret, go easy on me. You ought to. I'm at the end of my rope and feel that I'm suffocating. You don't want to be responsible for a person's destruction. You've got to let up. I feel I'm about to burst." His face had expanded. He struck a blow upon the tin and wood and nails of the wall of the booth. "You've got to let me breathe. If I should keel over, what then? And it's something I can never understand about you. How you can treat soemone like this whom you lived with so long. Who gave you the best of himself. Who tried. Who loved you." Merely to pronounce the word "love" made him tremble.

"Ah," she said with a sharp breath. "Now we're coming to it. How did you imagine it was going to be – big shot? Everything made smooth for you? I thought you were leading up to this."

She had not, perhaps, intended to reply as harshly as she did, but she brooded a great deal and now she could not forbear to punish him and make him feel pains like those she had to undergo.

He struck the wall again, this time with his knuckles, and he had scarcely enough air in his lungs to speak in a whisper, because his heart pushed upward with a frightful pressure. He got up and stamped his feet in the narrow enclosure.

"Haven't I always done my best?" he yelled, though his voice sounded weak and thin to his own ears. "Everything comes from me and nothing back again to me. There's no law that'll punish this, but you are committing a crime against me. Before God – and that's no joke. I mean that. Before God! Sooner or later the boys will know it."

In a firm tone, levelly, Margaret said to him, "I won't stand to be howled at. When you can speak normally and have something sensible to say I'll listen. But not to this." She hung up.

Wilhelm tried to tear the apparatus from the wall. He ground his teeth and seized the black box with insane digging fingers and made a stifled cry and pulled. Then he saw an elderly lady staring through the glass door, utterly appalled by him, and he ran from the booth, leaving a large amount of change on the shelf. He hurried down the stairs and into the street.

On Broadway it was still bright afternoon and the gassy air was almost motionless under the leaden spokes of sunlight, and sawdust footprints lay about the doorways of butcher shops and fruit stores. And the great, great crowd, the inexhaustible current of millions of every race and kind pouring out, pressing round, of every age, of every genius, possessors of every human secret, antique and future, in every face the refinement of one particular motive or essence – *I labour, I spend, I strive, I design, I love, I cling, I uphold, I give way, I envy, I long, I scorn, I die, I hide, I want*. Faster, much faster than any man could make the tally. The sidewalks were wider than any causeway; the street itself was immense, and it quaked and gleamed and it seemed to Wilhelm to throb at the last limit of endurance. And although the sunlight appeared like a broad tissue, its actual weight made him feel like a drunkard.

"I'll get a divorce if it's the last thing I do," he swore. "As for Dad – as for Dad – I'll have to sell the car for junk and pay the hotel. I'll have to go on my knees to Olive and say, "Stand by me a while. Don't let her win. Olive!" ' And he thought, I'll try to start again with Olive. In fact, I must. Olive loves me. Olive –

Beside a row of limousines near the kerb he thought he saw Dr Tamkin. Of course he had been mistaken before about the hat with the cocoa-coloured band and didn't want to make the same mistake twice. But wasn't that Tamkin who was speaking so earnestly, with pointed shoulders, to someone under the canopy of the funeral parlour? For this was a huge funeral. He looked for the singular face under the dark grey, fashionable hatbrim. There were two open cars filled with flowers, and a policeman tried to keep a path open to pedestrians. Right at the canopy-pole, now wasn't that that damned Tamkin talking away with a solemn face, gesticulating with an open hand?

"Tamkin!" shouted Wilhelm, going forward. But he was pushed to the side by a policeman clutching his nightstick at both ends, like a rolling pin. Wilhelm was even farther from Tamkin now, and swore under his breath at the cop who continued to press him back, back, belly and ribs, saying, "Keep it moving there, please," his face red with impatient sweat, his brows like red fur. Wilhelm said to him haughtily, "You shouldn't push people like this."

The policeman, however, was not really to blame. He had been 5 ordered to keep a way clear. Wilhelm was moved forward by the pressure of the crowd.

He cried, "Tamkin!"

But Tamkin was gone. Or rather, it was he himself who was carried from the street into the chapel. The pressure ended inside, where it was 10 dark and cool. The flow of fan-driven air dried his face, which he wiped hard with his handkerchief to stop the slight salt itch. He gave a sigh when he heard the organ notes that stirred and breathed from the pipes and he saw people in the pews. Men in formal clothes and black homburgs strode softly back and forth on the cork floor, up and down 15 the centre aisle. The white of the stained glass was like mother-of-pearl, the blue of the Star of David like velvet ribbon.

Well, thought Wilhelm, if that was Tamkin outside I might as well wait for him here where it's cool. Funny, he never mentioned he had a funeral to go to today. But that's just like the guy.

20 But within a few minutes he had forgotten Tamkin. He stood along the wall with others and looked toward the coffin and the slow line that was moving past it, gazing at the face of the dead. Presently he too was in this line, and slowly, slowly, foot by foot, the beating of his heart anxious, thick, frightening, but somehow also rich, he neared the coffin 25 and paused for his turn, and gazed down. He caught his breath when he looked at the corpse, and his face swelled, his eyes shone hugely with instant tears.

The dead man was grey-haired. He had two large waves of grey hair at the front. But he was not old. His face was long, and he had a bony 30 nose, slightly, delicately twisted. His brows were raised as though he had sunk into the final thought. Now at last he was with it, after the end of all distractions, and when his flesh was no longer flesh. And by this meditative look Wilhelm was so struck that he could not go away. In spite of the tinge of horror, and then the splash of heartsickness that he 35 felt, he could not go. He stepped out of line and remained beside the coffin; his eyes filled silently and through his still tears he studied the man as the line of visitors moved with veiled looks past the satin coffin towards the standing bank of lilies, lilacs, roses. With great stifling sorrow, almost admiration, Wilhelm nodded and nodded. On the surface, the dead man with his formal shirt and his tie and silk lapels and his powdered skin looked so proper; only a little beneath so – black, Wilhelm thought, so fallen in the eyes.

Standing a little apart, Wilhelm began to cry. He cried at first softly and from sentiment, but soon from deeper feeling. He sobbed loudly and his face grew distorted and hot, and the tears stung his skin. A man – another human creature, was what first went through his thoughts, but other and different things were torn from him. What'll I do? I'm stripped and kicked out... Oh, Father, what do I ask of you? What'll I do about the kids – Tommy, Paul? My children. And Olive? My dear! Why, why, why – you must protect me against that devil who wants my life. If you want it, then kill me. Take, take it, take it from me.

Soon he was past words, past reason, coherence. He could not stop. The source of all tears had suddenly sprung open within him, black, deep, and hot, and they were pouring out and convulsed his body, bending his stubborn head, bowing his shoulders, twisting his face, crippling the very hands with which he held the handkerchief. His efforts to collect himself were useless. The great knot of ill and grief in his throat swelled upward and he gave in utterly and held his face and wept. He cried with all his heart.

He, alone of all the people in the chapel, was sobbing. No one knew who he was.

One woman said, "Is that perhaps the cousin from New Orleans they were expecting?"

"It must be somebody real close to carry on so."

"Oh my, oh my! To be mourned like that," said one man and looked at Wilhelm's heavy shaken shoulders, his clutched face and whitened fair hair, with wide, glinting, jealous eyes.

"The man's brother, maybe?"

"Oh, I doubt that very much," said another bystander. "They're not alike at all. Night and day."

The flowers and lights fused ecstatically in Wilhelm's blind, wet eyes; the heavy sea-like music came up to his ears. It poured into him where he had hidden himself in the centre of a crowd by the great and happy oblivion of tears. He heard it and sank deeper than sorrow, through torn sobs and cries toward the consummation of his heart's ultimate need.

STUDY QUESTIONS

Chapter 1

1. Characterize the structure of this introductory chapter by commenting on the actual time-span of the action and on the different time-levels.
2. What is the significance of the repetition of the very first sentence ("When it came to concealing his troubles . . .") later in the text (p. 13, line 25 f.)?
3. Tommy abhors cynicism and irony (p. 15, line 26 f.). Why?
4. What do Dr. Tamkin, Artie and Maurice have in common?
5. Point out how Maurice Venice – in his film manager's jargon – sees Tommy.
6. Read Shakespeare's sonnet 73 and try to explain why Tommy suddenly remembers its last two lines (p. 12, line 9).

Chapter 2

1. Describe Tommy's behaviour when he is talking to his father. What does this reveal about their relationship?
2. What are Tommy's first impressions of Mr. Perls? Why does he see him like that?
3. What is it that annoys Tommy when he sees the IBM computer cards?
4. What forces Tommy to reveal himself before Mr. Perls in his conversation?
5. "The . . . peculiar burden of his existence lay upon him like . . a load" (p. 32, line 24 f.). Try and find other images of weight and burden in the first two chapters. What do they signify?
6. Collect the information that the reader has got about Dr. Tamkin in the first two chapters. What type of character seems to emerge from this evidence?

Chapter 3

1. "You make too much of your problems, said the doctor." (p. 37, line 35). Do you agree? Give reasons.
2. What does the allusion to Lincoln's Emancipation Proclamation (p. 40, line 23) mean?
3. Examine the images referring to strangling, suffocation, heavy breathing. Can you discover a connexion between these and the metaphors of weight that you have already analyzed?
4. Make a list of points in which Tommy and his father disagree.
5. Comment on Tommy's beg for help (p. 44, line 15). Support your ideas with an interpretation of Tommy's prayer at the end of chapter one.

Chapter 4

1. Tommy regards suffering as the "business of life", the "real business" (p. 46, line 7). What does he actually suffer from?
2. Explain why the manager of the brokerage office reminds Tommy of Rubin, the man at the newsstand (Chapter 1).
3. How is Tamkin's superiority expressed in his behaviour towards Tommy? In this connexion, study Tommy's description of Tamkin's outward appearance.
4. Give examples of, and comment on, Tamkin's obsession with psychiatric case histories and his predilection for "crazy" things. Why does he like to call himself a "psychological poet" and a "scientific man"?
5. Tamkin's distinction between the true soul and the pretender soul fascinates Tommy. Why?
6. "The waters of the earth are going to roll over me." (p. 63, line 10 f.). Can you find similar images of sinking and drowning in the preceding chapters? What do they express?

Chapter 5

1. Summarize and interpret Tommy's thoughts at the beginning of the chapter.
2. Tommy confesses that Dr. Tamkin gives him comfort. What is it in Tamkin that can influence Tommy in such a way?
3. Examine Tommy's description of his moment of insight in the underground corridor. What did he actually realize?
4. Why does the idea of the "larger body" occur to him while he is thinking about the complexity of a city like New York?
5. What are the basic ideas of Tamkin's concept of the here-and-now? Explain the connexion between this philosophy and the title of the book.
6. Do you understand why Tommy suddenly remembers the poem whose lines he gives us (p. 73, line 1 ff.)?

Chapter 6

1. The images of burden and drowning recur in this chapter. Explain their specific meaning in the context and give a reason why they are used here towards the end of the novel.
2. Tamkin's words about suffering seem to appeal to Tommy. Why?
3. Do you think Tommy's feelings about his own suffering are justified or only sentimental self-pity?
4. Point out Tommy's attitude to Mr. Rappaport and compare it to that in the preceding chapter.

Chapter 7

1. The old fiddler appears again in this chapter. Tommy feels that he is a kind of omen for him. Explain.
2. Bellow again uses the images of suffocation, carrying a burden and drowning – by now familiar to you – in this chapter. Analyze the context in which they appear and give a reason why the author uses them so frequently in this part of the novel.

3. Which parallels do you recognize in Tommy's conversations with his father and his wife?

4. Study the descriptions of the different places of the action in this chapter (steam-bath; telephone box; Broadway; chapel). Point out the similarities and explain what they mean for the novel.

5. What is the "ultimate need" of Tommy's heart?

6. Critics have given different interpretations of the funeral scene at the end of the book. Here are some of them for you to comment on:

   a) "Thus, at last he is able to confront that larger suffering which . . . has been the dead weight of existence pressing on him without any release or passion in him of understanding." *(A. Kazin)*

   b) "Thus, his final act reveals his ability to accept himself. It is in that moment of mystical illumination that Tommy can follow the advice of Tamkin and 'seize the day'." *(E. Harris)*

   c) "The weeping reveals him as a human being and links him to humankind." *(Ch. Eisinger)*

   d) "At the moment of death, his motion is toward existence, the vitality that defines and unites everyone, and his weeping is an acceptance of it and therefore an act of love toward life." *(M. Klein)*

   e) "The dead man is a reminder of the inevitable death of the self, at the same time he is a very specific omen to Tommy . . . Tommy's tears are both for humanity and himself." *(T. Tanner)*

CRITICAL COMMENTS ON "SEIZE THE DAY"

Study the following excerpts from books and articles on Bellow. Relate the ideas of the critics to the novel and give your own opinion.

1. *Death:* "The theme of death is introduced early in the work: a reference to Milton's *Lycidas* which Wilhelm recollects from his college course, constant allusions to Wilhelm's age and his father's fear of death. ... Death, we see, circulates in the golden arteries of our civilization ... This Bellow sees with terrible clarity; the abstract idea is rendered only too well." *(Hassan)*

2. *Failure:* "To fail to make the grade is a human achievement that teaches us what we are; it is an aspect of the myth that sustains America." *(Burgess)*

3. *The con-man:* "The age is full of great and dangerous monologists. He-whose-voice-is-heard is the dictator, demagogue, leader; he-who-makes-us-listen on the public address system or on the radio and whose monologue leads all others. The man who can make others listen is the man who has attained power." *(Bellow)*

4. *The anti-hero:* "... the anti-hero is the rebel-victim who is alienated from his culture and society. He has no power, no purpose, no prestige. And always his lot is martyrdom or unheroic defeat." *(Barksdale)*

5. *Suffering and redemption:* "Bellow is able to give us, step by step, the world we really live each day – and in the same movement to show us that the real suffering is always the suffering of not understanding, the deprivation of light." *(Kazin)*
   The sufferer "takes upon himself the unreason of human existence and redeems it by giving it form." *(Hassan)*

6. *American Jewish literature:* "In most of his work the Jewish fictionist in America seems strongly responsive to that sense of things which holds that the key situation of life is one of personal humiliation and the dominant emotion of human experience one of self-pity." *(DeMott)*

7. *Acceptance:* Bellow's novels are "sometimes read as fables of capitulation to mediocrity." *(Grogan)*

QUESTIONS FOR DISCUSSION

1. The title "Seize the Day" refers to the old literary motif of *carpe diem,* which has its origin in one of the odes of the Latin poet Horace. Discuss the choice of the title.

2. Bellow's heroes may be characterized with the titles of two of his novels, "Dangling Man" and "The Victim". Apply these terms to our novel. In what respect is Tommy a "dangling man" and what might he be a victim of?

3. The traditional comic character of Jewish jokes and stories is called – with a Yiddish term – *schlemiel.* This unheroic figure attracts misfortune without being destroyed by it. Tommy has often been called a modern *schlemiel.* Can you prove with evidence from the text that this statement is correct? Where do you see the causes of Tommy's misfortune and suffering?

4. Tommy's progress in his relationship to his world can be summed up as follows: humiliation – knowledge – love – reconciliation *(Hassan).* Can you trace these four stages of his development in the text?

5. There are several names for the hero of the novel, either adopted by himself or given to him by others. What are they? – A name is the mark of a person's identity. How do you explain this play with names in the novel?

6. Martin Luther King once wrote: "Freedom ist not won by a passive acceptance of suffering. Freedom is won by a struggle *against* suffering." Can you defend Tommy's acceptance of *his* suffering by contrasting his situation to that of the other great group of outsiders in America, the Blacks?

7. Here is a list of attributes that have been given to Dr. Tamkin: charlatan, visionary, parasite, schemer, con-man, pseudo-philosopher, manipulator, devil. Comment on the different shades of meaning and state which one you would choose. What, then, is the function of Tamkin in the novel?

8. *Seize the Day* is certainly not a funny novel. On the other hand, there is subtle humour to be found. Can you pick out comic scenes and characterize the type of humour displayed in them?

9. Apart from the images that have been mentioned in the "Study

Questions" (sinking, drowning, weight, burden, suffocation), there are some other fields of images, e. g. those referring to deformity and ageing. Make a list of examples. Can you discover a system in Bellow's use of metaphoric language?

10. The successful individual is commonly regarded as the representa-tive of the "American way of life". Can *Seize the Day* also be seen as an example of social criticism?

SELECTED BIBLIOGRAPHY

Bischoff, Peter. *Saul Bellows Romane: Entfremdung und Suche*. Bonn 1975.

Bischoff, Peter. "Protagonist und Umwelt in Saul Bellows Romanen: ein Forschungsbericht". *Literatur in Wissenschaft und Unterricht*, 8 (No. 4, 1975), p. 257–276.

Hasenclever, Walter. *Saul Bellow: eine Monographie*. Köln 1978.

Klein, Marcus. "A Discipline of Nobility: Saul Bellow's Fiction". Reprinted in (1) Malin, p. 92–113.

(1) Malin, Irving (ed.). *Saul Bellow and the Critics*. New York 1967.

(2) Malin, Irving. "Seven Images". Reprinted in (1) Malin, p. 142–176.

Mathis, James C. "The Theme of *Seize the Day*". *Critique*, 7 (Spring-Summer, 1965), p. 43–45.

Rothermel, Wolfgang P. "Saul Bellow". *Amerikanische Literatur der Gegenwart in Einzeldarstellungen*, ed. Martin Christadler. Stuttgart 1973, p. 69–104.

Rovit, Earl. *Saul Bellow*. Minneapolis 1967. University of Minnesota Pamphlets on American Writers, no. 65.

Rovit, Earl (ed.). *Saul Bellow: A Collection of Critical Essays*. Englewood Cliffs, N. J. 1975.

Schiffer, Reinhold. "Modern Writers: Saul Bellow". *Praxis des Neusprachlichen Unterrichts,* 19 (no. 1, 1972), p. 58–62.

Tanner, Tony. *Saul Bellow*. Edinburgh and London 1965. Writers and Critics Series.

Trowbridge, Clinton. "Water Imagery in *Seize the Day*". *Critique*, 9 (1967), p. 62–73.

Weiss, Daniel. "Caliban on Prospero: A Psychoanalytic Study on the Novel *Seize the Day* by Saul Bellow". Reprinted in (1) Malin, p. 114–141.

ANNOTATIONS

Abbreviations: adj. adjective — **adv.** adverb — **AE.** American English — **arch.** archaic (old use) — **cf.** compare — **coll.** colloquial — **dial.** dialect — **G.** German — **L.** Latin — **n.** noun — **obj.** object — **o.s.** oneself — **pl.** plural — **sl.** slang — **s.o.** someone — **s.th.** something — **subj.** subject — **vb.** verb — **vulg.** vulgar use

Introduction

Page 3:

3 **Walt Whitman** (1819–1892) one of the great American poets ("Leaves of Grass")

5 **Quebec** [kwiˈbek]

10 **anthropology** [ænθrəˈpɔlədʒi] science of man

11 **post-graduate** after the B.A. degree

14 **reputation** G. Ruf, Ansehen

16 **Creative Writing** university courses in which the technique of writing fiction is taught

24 **to assume** to believe

28 **relevance** importance.

Page 4:

3 **account** report

8 **to affirm** to react positively to

9 **victim** G. Opfer (person)

10 **humiliation** G. Erniedrigung

13 **nihilism** [ˈnaiilizm] **alienation** [eiljəˈneiʃn] the state of being isolated from one's environment

14 **accommodation** G. Anpassung

21 **schlemiel** [ʃləˈmiːl] (AE sl.) G. Pechvogel

25 **theoreticians** [θiəreˈtiʃənz] persons basing their ideas on theory rather than on practice

26 **con(fidence) man** swindler

30 **tottering** unstable, shaky

31 **to relinquish** to give up, to surrender

Chapter 1

Page 5:

3 **to conceal** to hide

6 **extra** an actor who takes a very small part in a play

9 **mezzanine** [ˈmezəniːn] storey between two floors

18 **to billow** to rise like waves

19 **drapes** curtain hanging in folds

21 **to light** to come to rest **marquee** [mɑːˈkiː] a rooflike shelter above a theatre entrance

25 **the Seventies, Eighties, and Nineties** area between the 70th and 90th Streets in Manhattan

28 **subway grating** frame of metal bars covering an underground passage

29 **dime store** (AE.) shop selling cheap goods (dime = 10c coin).

Page 6:

3 **morale** [mɔ'rɑːl] the moral condition of a person

10 **to presage** [pri'seidʒ] to predict, G. vorhersagen

14 **lacy** G. spitzenartig

15 **to furl** to roll

17 **cuffs** the band at the end of a sleeve

22 **Stanford White** famous American architect

24 **fretwork** G. Gitterwerk
festoon [fes'tuːn] G. (hier: eisernes) Laufgehänge

27 **slate** G. Schiefer
tufa G. Tuffstein

29 **cavernous** ['kævənəs] hollow and deep

33 **knocked-out** (coll.) first rate, excellent

34 **Saks** department store in Manhattan

35 **Jack Fagman** brand of a shirt

Page 7:

6 **freshman** (AE. coll.) first year student
racoon G. Waschbär

7 **beanie** (AE.) little cap worn by children and college freshmen

13 **bucks** (AE. coll.) dollars

15 **falling out** a serious quarrel

18 **for that matter** as far as that is concerned

22 **pretty sharp** (AE. coll.) rather (very) elegant

25 **damask** ['dæməsk] G. Damast
embossed decorated with a raised ornament

32 **hippopotamus** [hipə'pɔtəməs] G. Nilpferd

34 **stump teeth** remnants of teeth

Page 8:

13 **gin game** (AE.) gin rummy, a variation of canasta

20 **chump** (sl.) fool

25 **Trib** (coll.) New York Herald Tribune

26 **closing quotations** last reports from the stock market

31 **cigarette butt** the end of a cigarette

32 **dental floss** soft thread for cleaning the spaces between the teeth.

Page 9:

1 **lard** fat of pigs

2 **commodities market** [kə'mɔditiːz] G. Produktenbörse

5 **margin payment** security deposit as a provision against loss

8 **uptown** referring to the northern part of Manhattan

14 **alertness** being very attentive

18 **soy beans** G. Sojabohnen
hide skin of a larger animal (cow, buffalo etc.)

23 **bulging** protruding

24 **dough** (sl.) [dəu] money

28 **way** (AE. coll.) adv. far

Page 10:

7 **joint return** G. gemeinsame Einkommenssteuererklärung

9 **bracket** income bracket, grouping of the income according to the amount received

31 **persuasive** able to convince others

34 **detachment** lack of interest

35 **affable** [ˈæfəbl] easy to talk to

Page 11:

11 **Puget Sound** [ˈPjuːdʒit] an arm of the Pacific, in the state of Washington

12 **Giants, Dodgers** names of popular and famous baseball teams

20 **schedule** [ˈʃedjuːl; AE. ˈsk-] timetable

21 **kin** relatives

30 **immaculate** absolutely clean

31 **he has all his buttons** (coll.) his intellect is clear

34 **to pamper** to spoil s.o. with extreme care

Page 12:

2 **to prime s.o.** G. jmd. „bearbeiten"

9 ... **love that well** ... last line of sonnet 73 by William Shakespeare
thou (arch.) [ðau] you
ere (arch.) [ɛə] before

10 **involuntary** [inˈvɔləntəri] against one's will

12 **this thou perceivest** ... line from sonnet 73
perceivest (arch.) 2nd person singular present of "perceive"

21 **accomplishment** [-ˈkʌ-] achievement

22 **yet once more** ... first line from a long poem by John Milton (17th century) called **Lycidas** [ˈlisidæs] about a friend who was drowned in the Irish Sea
ye (arch.) you (plural)
laurels G. Lorbeeren

24 **sunk though he be** ... from Milton's **Lycidas**

25 **to sway** to move to and fro

28 **alumnus** (AE.) [əˈlʌmnəs] former student of a university
Penn State Pennsylvania State University

29 **sophomore** (AE. coll.) second year student

30 **B. S. degree** academic title of a **Bachelor of Science**

31 **Bryn Mawr** [brin ˈmɔr] famous women's college in Pennsylvania

34 **to brag** to speak boastfully

35 **sales executive** manager in the sales department of a firm

Page 13:

1 **up in the five figures** (coll.) from ten to a hundred thousand dollars a year

7 **hypocrite** [ˈhipəkrit] G. Heuchler

10 **snow job** (AE. sl.) persuasion through exaggeration

16 **cords** G. Stimmbänder

17 **pal** (AE. coll.) good friend

23 **to droop** hang down

31 **monicker** (AE. sl.) (nick)name

34 **talent scout** person in show business searching for future stars.

Page 14:

5 **to tilt** to turn into a sloping position

9 **flivver** (AE.) old, small, or cheap car

slicker (AE.) long, waterproof raincoat

10 **Coke dates** (AE. coll.) rendezvous with a girl and with Coca-Cola as a drink

he had had college he was fed up with going to college

14 **intricate** extremely complicated

22 **jerk** (AE. sl.) a naive person

31 **to loiter** to move about aimlessly

38 **to warp** [wɔ:p] to bend.

Page 15:

5 **to pan out** to succeed

15 **mole** G. Muttermal

32 **chicken** (AE. sl.) coward

congestion [-dʒ-] being overcrowded

33 **rat race** (coll.) hectic activity

phony (sl.) adj. pseudo-, sham, not genuine

bugger (sl.) idiot

35 **to run for** (an office) to be a candidate.

Page 16:

4 **husky** hoarse

double-breasted suit with two rows of buttons

5 **chalk-striped** G. mit breiten Streifen

8 **to dwarf** to appear small in size

9 **Golden Grimes** type of apple

11 **unwarped** [-wɔ:-] stretched

18 **credentials** written evidence of authority

19 **stationery** writing paper

22 **racket** (sl.) illegal business

25 **fishy** (coll.) of questionable character

27 **distributor** a person or firm organizing the distribution of films among the cinema owners

31 **to size s.o. up** (coll.) to judge s.o.

dinky (AE. coll.) of small size

37 **ruddy** red, reddish.

Page 17:

6 **brassière ad** [ˈbræsjəˈæd] G. Büstenhalter-Anzeige

15 **to pull one's leg** to play a trick on s.o.

to give a tease to provoke s.o.

16 **to horse around** (coll.) to fool around

21 **to get off on the wrong foot with s. o.** G. es mit jmd. verderben

37 **thigh** G. Schenkel

38 **mantilla** Spanish head scarf.

Page 18:

1 **peppy** (coll.) lively, vigorous

3 **broad** (AE. sl.) woman, girl

8 **terry-cloth** G. Frottéstoff

10 **Malibu** suburb of Los Angeles

15 **to strike a bell** to remind s. o. of s. th.

33 ff. **Conway Tearle, Jack Mulhall, George Bancroft, George Raft, Edward G. Robinson, James Cagney, William Powell, Buddy Rogers** American film stars

34 **ruggeder** [ˈrʌgidə] unusual comparative of **rugged;** wrinkled

38 **sideburns** G. „Koteletten",
Backenbart.

Page 19:
1 **fly-in-your-face role**
directness,
aggressiveness
2 **cabbie** (AE. sl.) taxi-driver
punch a blow with the fist
4 **suave** (swɑːv) agreeable,
polite
5 **sax** (coll.) saxophone
8 **to get stood up** (AE. coll.) G.
im Stich gelassen werden
12 **provider** breadwinner of the
family
16 **to cast** to give a role to an
actor
17 **defiant** rebellious
21 **stuff** (coll.) nonsense
22 **to plug along** (coll.) to work
steadily
24 **Swanson** Gloria Swanson,
American film star
25 **bunk** (AE. sl.) nonsense,
humbug
27 **billion** (AE.) G. Milliarde
28 **bud** (AE. coll.) friend, chap.

Page 20:
1 **stapled together** G.
zusammengeheftet
4 **to shoot the works** (AE. sl.)
to try to achieve s. th. by
spending all resources
26 **infallible** absolutely sure
28 **about-face** (AE.) quick turning
of one's head
29 **sound-track** G. Tonspur der
Filmstreifens
32 **vault** (of the chest) G.
Wölbung des Brustkorbs.

Page 21:
10 **orderly** hospital attendant
11 **under indictment** [in'dait-]
being accused of
12 **pandering** G. Kuppelei
17 **fall guy, dupe, sucker** (AE.
sl.) person who is easily deceived
or fooled
32 **scope** range of activity or
thinking
foreboding omen
37 **clunk** (AE. sl.) fool

Page 22:
17 **to brood** to work on s. th.
with persistence
22 **pathetic** [pə'θetik] totally
confused, mixed up.

Chapter 2

Page 23:
5 **brokerage account** G. Konto
beim Makler
10 **SEC** **S**ecurities and **E**xchange
Commission, G.
Börsenkontrollbehörde der
Regierung
13 **tab** (coll.) unpaid bill
22 **insinuation** indirect hint
30 **Gosh** (AE. sl.) God
38 **to wag** to move from side to
side.

Page 24:
5 **to interne** (AE.) to work as an assistant doctor in a hospital to complete one's training
10 **to hoist up** to pull up
pants (AE.) trousers
11 **to jitter** (AE.) to move nervously
30 **to twitch** to move with a sudden motion.

Page 25:
9 **ostensibly** seemingly, not really
18 **gut** (usually plural) (here:) belly
22 **clunk** (sl.) stupid person
28 **post-dated cheque** cheque with a later date than the true date, so that it cannot be cashed at the moment
30 **policy** G. (Versicherungs-) Police
37 **to punch out** to stamp out on computer cards
38 **IBM** International Business Machines Corporation.

Page 26:
3 **sucker** (AE. coll.) inexperienced person
4 **dough, scratch** (sl.) money
12 **at the end of one's rope** at the end of one's means
17 **pastry** ['peistri] sweet baked food, pie, tart
19 **bay** compartment in a large room, set off by walls
25 **private-eye school** detectives' training school
reducing parlour institution

where people are trained to lose weight
27 **hoop** ringlike object or figure
28 **murkiness** thick with haze
30 **putty** ['pʌti] G. Kitt
31 **enamel** [i'næməl] G. Email
32 **tardy** slow-moving
37 **bias** subjective point of view.

Page 27:
1 **frazzle-faced** looking completely exhausted
2 **moustache** [məs'tɑːʃ] G. Schnurrbart
5 **stainless** resisting rust
8 **suppliance** ['sʌpliəns] appeal, begging
10 **ground to the quick** moved hard against one another
12 **to wince** to shrink back in pain
14 **hosiery wholesaler** ['həuʒəri] G. Großhändler in Strickwaren
17 **anaesthetist** [æ'niːsθitist]
18 **Mount Sinai** ['sainai] name of a hospital
25 **on the outs** (AE. coll.) on bad terms.

Page 28:
1 **stimulant** medicine that activates physical processes
2 **depressant** medicine that lowers the vital activities
anodyne ['ænəudain] pain-relieving medicine
analeptic medicine giving strength after a disease
3 **Luminal** brand of sleeping-pills
4 **Pervitin, Benzedrine** brands of stimulating medicine

9 **alternate parking** (AE.) special parking system in American cities

11 **to tow away** [təu] to pull (a car)

14 **to sting, stung** (coll.) to catch in the act

ticket notice of an offence against traffic regulations

16 **in your line** (coll.) in your job

17 **lunatic** ['lu:nətik] an insane person

20 **expense account** G. Spesenkonto

garage ['gærɑ:ʒ, -dʒ]

26 **gear** G. Gang (beim Auto)

33 **cemetery** ['semitri] graveyard

36 **hoodlums** (sl.) gangsters

37 **sledge-hammer** Vorschlaghammer

smack (coll.) adv. suddenly and violently.

Page 29:

1 **to cremate** to burn a dead body

5 **Estonian** (adj.) from Estonia, G. Estland

12 **sedative** ['sedətiv] medicine lowering physical activity G. Beruhigungsmittel

21 **respiratory centre** ['respirətri] G. Atemzentrum

34 **Jungle-Gym** (AE.) G. (Spielzeug-) Strickleiter

35 **seesaw** G. Wippe

Page 30:

7 **blasted** (coll.) damned

19 **to hug** to hold s. th. or s. o. tightly

relish liking, sympathy

22 **dummy** (coll.) a stupid person

23 **chicken** (coll.) rubbish, nonsense

25 **congestion** unnatural pressure of blood

37 **to root** (AE. coll.) to be a fan of a sports team

38 **Duke** nick-name of a popular American baseball-player.

Page 31:

3 **quart** liquid measure, about one litre

4 **insomnia** sleeplessness

10 **jerkily** with a sudden movement

18 **executive standing** position of an executive

to mortify to hurt s. o.'s pride

29 **feud** [fju:d] quarrel

34 **WPA** (AE.) **W**ork **P**rojects **A**dministration; U. S. agency which in the late thirties gave public work to people to relieve national unemployment

38 **translucent** permitting light to pass through but not transparent like glass.

Page 32:

3 **hearing-aid** G. Hörgerät

doodad (AE. coll.) superfluous thing, gimmick

25 **accretion** [æ'kri:ʃən] increase by gradual addition.

Page 33:

3 **mango** tropical fruit

acre square measure, about half a hectare

8 **Leonard Lyons** popular American column-writer

13 **strapped** (AE. coll.) penniless

16 **to haemorrhage** [ˈhemərɪdʒ]
to bleed strongly

28 **psychologist** [saiˈkɔlədʒist]

29 **psychiatrist** [saiˈkaiətrist].

Page 34:

5 **Fortune** American magazine

6 **clipping** article cut out from a newspaper

8 **operator** (sl.) swindler, charlatan

16 **to trigger** to cause a reaction

20 **Albany** capital of the state of New York

31 **power of attorney** [əˈtəːni] G. Vollmacht.

Chapter 3

Page 35:

10 **ailment** illness

12 **to be put on notice** to be expected to give one's opinion

14 **muffin** [-ʌ-] small, round bread eaten with butter

22 **to drag o. s.** to move slowly, with effort

24 **mountainous** [ˈmauntinəs] reminding of a mountain
slovenly (adj.) [-ʌ] G. schlampig

25 **delicacy** [ˈdelikəsi]

32 **wicker chair** G. Korbsessel

33 **slug** type of snail
hollyhocks G. Herbstrosen.

Page 36:

3 **vexatious** [vekˈseiʃəs] troublesome, annoying

5 **congested** overburdened

6 **clutch** a group of things close together
to lay off (AE. sl.) to stop annoying

7 **pal** (AE. coll.) chap, friend

8 **prompting** lines given to an actor as a help during the performance

25 **hydrotherapy** [haidrəˈθerəpi]

massage [ˈmæsaːʒ]

27 **barbiturate** [baːˈbitjurit] medicine lowering physical functions

38 **potsy** (AE.) play in the sandbox
skiprope G. Seilspringen

Page 37:

19 **boost** (AE.) lift, increase

29 **droop** hanging position

30 **to intimate** [ˈintimeit] to suggest

Page 38:

7 **to file a joint tax return** G. eine gemeinsame Steuererklärung abgeben

14 **benevolence** [biˈnevələns]

15 **beneficiary** [beniˈfiʃəri] person who has the advantage of s. th.

24 **ferny** G. farnartig.

Page 39:

25 **to indulge o. s. in** to allow o. s. the pleasure of.

Page 40:

15 **suffocation** [sʌfəˈkeiʃən] having difficulties in breathing

16 **apoplexy** [ˈæpəpleksi] G. Schlaganfall

18 **bunk** (AE. coll.) nonsense

19 **voodoo** [ˈvuːduː] here: black magic

23 **Emancipation Proclamation** [imænsiˈpeiʃən] proclamation by President Lincoln freeing the slaves (1863)

27 **bum** (AE. sl.) tramp.

Page 41:

27 **dry goods** textile material.

Page 42:

10 **to stick it out** (AE. coll.) to stay with s. th. to the end

23 **fall guy** (AE. sl.) person who is easily fooled

35 **pallor** paleness of the face.

Page 43:

14 **gross** [grəus] lacking in good manners; vulgar

25 **to rust out** to wear out by use.

Page 44:

9 **hazy** not distinct

14 **surf** foamy water on top of a wave

27 **woodchuck** G. Murmeltier (North America)

31 **service** army

33 **exemption** [igˈzempʃən] G. Befreiung vom Wehrdienst

34 **Pacific theatre** G. Kriegsschauplatz des Pazifik.

Page 45:

34 **corny** (coll.) G. kitschig, abgedroschen.

Page 46:

9 **to quell tears** to suppress weeping

15 **to poke** to push
to blunder to make a mistake
to go by fits and starts to act from time to time
to fall upon the thorns of life line from Shelley's **Ode to the West Wind** (early 19th century): "O! lift me as a wave, a leaf, a cloud!/I fall upon the thorns of life! I bleed!"

16 **thorn** [θɔːn] G. Dorn
finally sink beneath that watery floor another allusion to Milton's poem **Lycidas**

17 **tough luck** bad luck
riddance relief

24 **in dutch** (AE. sl.) in trouble

31 **sore** (AE. coll.) angry, annoyed

36 **splotched** stained.

Page 47:

3 **obsessional** dominated by an idea

4 **to figure out** (AE. coll.) to understand, to grasp

19 **district attorney** (AE.) Staatsanwalt

25 **in abeyance** [əˈbeiəns] temporarily suspended, not in use

28 **pimp** G. Zuhälter

31 **fatality** misfortune resulting in a catastrophe.

Page 48:

12 **to convulse** shake heavily
aberration utter confusion

16 **to bounce** (of a cheque; coll.) G. „platzen"

36 **fumbler** person who acts clumsily, without success.

Page 49:

8 **asset** ['æset] G. Besitz, Vermögen

18 **level** (adj.) balanced, with a calm judgement

33 **to figure** (AE. coll.) to think about, to conclude.

Page 50:

2 **grain** G. Getreide

4 **to get a kick out of s. th.** (coll.) to get excitement

8 **hood** (AE.) cover over the engine of a car; bonnet

11 **jeer** expression of mock

31 **sordid** depraved, degraded

34 **patriarch** ['peitriɑ:k].

Page 51:

10 **occiput** ['ɔksipʌt] (technical term) back part of the head

12 **pagoda** G. Pagode

13 **devious** ['di:vjəs] not straightforward, not honest

22 **exertion** [ig'zɔ:ʃən] great effort

33 **bull** (AE. sl.) nonsense.

Page 52:

5 **to disembark** to leave a ship, to go ashore

8 **flaunting** attracting attention to o. s.
boisterous [-ɔi-] rough and noisy

20 **duress** [dju'res] violence or threat used to force s. o. to do s. th.
phony fake, not genuine

30 **licking** (coll.) defeat

36 **I took a licking in hides and coffee** I lost my money speculating in skins and coffee

38 **wizard** ['wizəd] magician, conjurer.

Page 53:

22 **premonition** forewarning

27 **killer-diller** (AE. sl.) joker, clown

36 **true confession magazine** magazine specializing in publishing private, intimate, "true" stories.

Page 54:

16 **fee** money doctors get for their service

25 **broomstick skirt** long and tight skirt

27 **pathology** [pæ'θɔlədʒi] case of a serious disease

28 **seizure** ['si:ʒə] sudden attack of epilepsy

33 **sibling** ['sibliŋ] brother or sister.

Page 55:

15 **Toledo** city in the state of Ohio

34 **big shot** (AE. coll.) famous influential person
for the heck of it (AE. coll.) just for fun

38 **to tip s. o. off** (coll.) to give s. o. a. warning, a hint.

Page 56:

8 **to sue s. o.** to bring a civil action against s. o. in court

9 **suit** legal case

14 **crook** (coll.) swindler

15 **jerk** (coll.) crazy person

36 **to get the drift** to understand the general meaning

38 **spicule** ['spaikju:l] G. kleine Ähre

Page 57:

12 **to grovel** ['grɔvl] to lie down in front of s. o., to beg for mercy

13 **on the sly** secretly

17 **flapjack** small flat cake

20 **hinge** in anatomy a joint where movement of a part of the body is possible

23 **pretender** person who likes to make believe

33 **charity drive** G. Wohltätigkeitsversammlung.

Page 58:

14 **to slay** to kill, to murder

15 **to gyp** [dʒip] **s. o.** (AE. coll.) to deceive s. o.

19 **parasite** ['pærəsait]

20 **ever take up . . .** (coll.) did you ever . . .

21 **parasitology** [pærəsai'tɔlədʒi] science of the parasites

26 **purgatory** ['pə:gətri] hell, place of suffering; G. Fegefeuer

27 **de profundis** (L.) from the depths

37 **aerial** ['ɛəriəl] antenna

38 **Korzybski, Aristotle, Freud, Sheldon** famous philosophers and scientists.

Page 59:

1 **layman** amateur, not an expert

27 **to crave** to long for eagerly.

Page 60:

5 **menu** ['menju:]

14 **pug** G. Mops

23 **to welsh** to go away without paying (of bookmasters) G. s. um etw. drücken

28 **throbbing** beating rapidly

37 **locust** ['ləukəst] G. Heuschrecke.

Page 61:

1 **ruled** (of paper) marked with lines

3 **vs** versus (against)

4 ff. **thee, thyself, thou, thy, ye, thine** (arch.) you (obj.), yourself, you (subj.), your, you (plural), your

7 **trinity** G. Dreifaltigkeit

8 **why-forth** what for (artificial word)

to tarry (arch.) to wait, to hesitate

10 **narry** (dial.: nary) never

18 **Mt** Mount

serenity [si'reniti] state of being calm

Serenity G. Durchlaucht (title)

21 **claptrap** insincere language

29 **flash powder** G. Blitzlichtpulver

Page 62:

2 **to square with** to agree with **Planck's Constant** G. Plancksches Wirkungsquantum

4 **figure of speech** G. rhetorische Figur

12 **-k it all!** (sl.) damn it all (for vulg. **fuck it all!**)

36 **lavish** generous

Chapter 5

Page 63:

13 **scoop** big spoon

15 **lilacs** [ˈlailəks]

25 **to relinquish** to give up.

Page 64:

2 **margin** [ˈmɑːdʒin] (here: margin payment) security deposit

19 **aisle** [ɑil] gangway

24 **seersucker** thin material with a crinkled surface

Vandyke [ˈvændaik] short, pointed beard

32 **junior** (AE.) third year student

37 **to clear** to earn.

Page 65:

10 **to foot the bill** (coll.) to pay it, to agree to

13 **aside** (n.) words spoken so as not to be heard by others

17 **grand** (AE. sl.) a thousand dollars

after taxes after taxes have been deducted

26 **to squander** [-ɔ-] to waste

29 **parenthetical** (here:) nonchalant

36 **receipt** [riˈsiːt] written acknowledgement of having received s. th.

37 **debit slip** G. Lastschriftzettel.

Page 66:

8 **takes some of the sting out** relieves us a little bit

14 **slump** [-ʌ-] period of low prices on the stock market

18 **.24** G. 0,24

23 **to whir** [wəː] to move quickly with a humming sound.

Page 67:

17 **plunger** [-dʒ-] unscrupulous speculator

23 **corduroy** [ˈkɔːdəroi] G. Kord

24 **Clyde's** expensive clothing shop in New York

29 **to defraud** to cheat, to deceive.

Page 68:

24 **hoop** ringlike form

29 **double-header** (AE.) two matches in a row between the same teams

34 **freak** unusual, anomalous object

36 **lurid** ghostly, pale.

Page 69:

10 **onrush** strong forward flow; G. Ansturm

13 **hard-on** (sl.) erection

25 **sinister** threatening

26 **to ramble** to grow in an unsystematic way

28 **coop** cage for small animals, e. g. hens

30 **shit** (sl.) excrements

33 **cartilage** [ˈkɑːtilidʒ] G. Knorpel

38 **memorandum,** pl. **-a** note.

Page 70:

10 **Yom Kippur** [jɔmˈkipə] high Jewish holiday

13 **Yiskor** [ˈjiskə] Jewish service for commemorating the dead

28 **to whiff** to smoke in short puffs

35 **chicken-sexer** person who finds out the sex of chickens
to hatch to cause young animals to be born by brooding.

Page 71:

15 **pungency** ['pʌndʒənsi] biting smell
21 **tumbler** G. Scheiben auf der elektronischen Anzeigetafel
28 **to scoff** to mock
34 **to ride** (here:) to join the game.

Page 72:

14 **flu** (coll.) influenza, G. Grippe
16 **bagpipes** musical instrument, especially popular among Scots

18 **to drown s. o. out** to be louder than s. o. else
19 **kilt** short skirt worn by men in the Scottish Highlands
33 **to seize** (here:) G. pfänden.

Page 73:

1 **Come then, Sorrow ...** text of a lullaby ['lʌləbai], a song to lull a child to sleep
3 **babe** (arch.) baby
15 **to con** to deceive (from **con man,** G. Hochstapler)
18 **to fray** to make worn, with loose ends.

Chapter 6

Page 74:

1 **sumptuous** ['sʌmptjuəs] superb, excellent
9 **crackers** thin, salty biscuits
14 **mascara** [mæs'kɑːrə], **henna** cosmetics (vb. from these n.)
23 **pot roast** dish of meat
27 **to stall** [-ɔː-] to distract
33 **to fix o. s. up** to reorganize o. s.
38 **guardedly** watchfully.

Page 75:

5 **scheme** [skiːm] plan, trick
15 **shrewd** showing common sense
24 **to writhe** to twist the body in pain
28 **soprano** [sə'prɑːnəu].

Page 76:

4 **to blast** (coll.) to damn
15 **to whine** long complaining cry, e. g. of dogs
25 **osteopath** ['ɔstiəupæθ] Osteopath, Knochenheilkundiger
33 **to hitch** to fasten by means of a hook
garters elastic strap for holding up a stocking
slip underskirt, petticoat.

Page 77:

2 **Reno** city in the state of Nevada where couples are easily divorced
6 **rich** (coll.) amusing, absurd
8 **scornful** full of contempt

18 **Santa Barbara** city on the southern coast of California

20 **lush** (AE. sl.) drunkard

26 **Provincetown, Cape Cod** seaside resort in the state of Massachusetts

34 f. **bogus** [ˈbəugəs] **humbug** [ˈhʌmbʌg] deceitful person, swindler.

Page 78:

6 **charlatan** [ˈʃɑːlətən]

16 **receptor** (technical term) end organ specialized to be sensitive to stimulation; G. Sinnesorgane, die auf äußere Reize reagieren (Rezeptoren)

17 **pincushion** [ˈpinkuʃən] G. Nadelkissen.

Page 79:

6 **Theodore Roosevelt** (1858–1919) former President of the U.S.

12 **morbid** unhealthy **innately** from birth on

23 **to be deprived of** be robbed of

32 **adultery** [əˈdʌltəri] G. Ehebruch

37 **faker** swindler, deceiver.

Page 80:

16 **maladjustment** bad adjustment.

Page 81:

18 **pelvis** G. Becken **suspenders** (AE.) pair of braces to keep up trousers **to gape** to become wide open.

Page 82:

2 **spoke** G. Speiche

4 **to be ascared** (coll. for scared) to fear

5 **dope** (AE. sl.) drugs

6 **hopped up** (AE. sl.) drugged

20 **poky** (AE. coll.) slow

37 **When we licked Spain** (coll.) when we defeated Spain, in the Spanish-American War in 1898

38 **gob** (AE. coll.) seaman in the U.S. Navy.

Page 83:

1 **battle of San Juan Hill** in July 1898

3 **kerb** edge of a pavement

7 **sentry** guard

12 **big-shot** (adj.) leading, influential (coll.)

19 **snap** (coll.) energy, liveliness

22 **T. R.** initials of Teddy Roosevelt

32 **slot** G. Schlitz.

Page 84:

12 **numb** [nʌm] without ability to feel

21 **You get hit?** (AE. sl.) Are you in great trouble?

27 **collar bone** bone between the shoulder and the breast-bone

30 **slump** period in which the prices of stocks fall

32 **did not dare turn** (AE.) did not dare **to** turn.

Page 85:

14 **latch** handle of the door.

Chapter 7

Page 85:

28 **hoary** [-ɔ:-] grey with age

30 **to dodge** to move quickly to avoid a difficulty

34 **mink stole** G. Nerzstola
leash line for holding a dog
high-strung highly nervous.

Page 86:

8 **to snub s. o.** try to ignore s. o.

16 **double-pronged** looking like a fork

23 **Hoboken** [ˈhəuˌbəukən] sea-port in New Jersey, opposite New York City
azure [ˈæʒə] sky-blue colour

25 **bluff** steep coast-line
berth place where a ship lies at anchor
tug G. Schleppdampfer

26 **cordage** ropes of a ship
brackish unpleasant

28 **scale** G. Tonleiter

29 **ledge** shelf coming out of the wall

33 **masseur** [mæˈsə:].

Page 87:

2 **to flicker** to rub with quick motions
receiver part of the telephone held to the ear

10 **to swirl** move around with a twisting motion

18 **fringes** G. Fransen

28 **separate** [ˈseprit] (adj.)

33 **contagion** [kənˈteidʒən] communication of disease by contact.

Page 88:

14 **wintergreen oil** G. bei Massagen als Gegenreizmittel benutztes Öl.

Page 89:

17 **slob** (AE. sl.) untidy person

23 **adjacent** [əˈdʒeisənt] next

33 **to spill out** to take out and scatter it

34 **to dial** to call a telephone number.

Page 90:

18 **nickels, dimes, quarters** (AE. coll.) five-cent, ten-cent, 25-cent pieces

28 **to patch things up with s. o.** (coll.) to try to find an arrangement with s. o.

34 **eligible for** [-dʒ-] legally entitled to.

Page 91:

5 **bangs** hair combed forward over the forehead

12 **stock** share; G. Aktie

20 **to rave** to talk furiously.

Page 92:

2 **she drove it home** (coll.) she made him feel it

9 **tuition** [tjuˈiʃən] money paid for professional training

17 **to keel over** to have a sudden breakdown

25 **to forbear** to keep back, to withhold, to refrain from

36 **level** (adj.) balanced, calm.

Page 93:

8 **leaden** ['ledən]

15 **to make the tally** to count, to register, to reckon up

16 **causeway** raised footpath

21 **junk** [dʒʌŋk] worthless material

29 **canopy** G. Baldachin

36 **nightstick** (AE.) truncheon carried by policemen; G. Gummiknüppel

38 **cop** (AE. coll.) policeman.

Page 94:

13 **pews** fixed benches in the church

14 **homburg** hat with a soft

crown

31 **with it** with all the trouble left behind

34 **tinge of horror** [-dʒ-] slight degree of horror.

Page 95:

2 **lapel** [lə'pel] part of a suit folded back on the breast

14 **coherence** [kəu'hiərəns] logical connection

17 **to bow** [bau]

29 **to glint** flashing brightly

33 **to fuse** to mix

36 **oblivion** being forgotten

37 **consummation** completion, perfection.

Critical Comments

Page 101:

9 **to render** to communicate

10 **to make the grade** to have success

11 **myth** [miθ] G. Mythos
to sustain to support

15 **public address system** system

of loudspeakers

22 **redemption** G. Erlösung

25 **deprivation** loss

27 **to redeem** to deliver

34 **mediocrity** [midi'ɔkriti] G. Mittelmäßigkeit.

Questions for Discussion

Page 102:

12 **evidence** proof

16 **reconciliation** [rekənsili'eiʃən]

G. Versöhnung

34 **subtle** ['sʌtl] delicate.